PROJE(

15 Stories

To Gibbo

I miss you Brother

INTRODUCTION

Firstly, thank you for buying this book. If you didn't buy it, thank you for borrowing or stealing it. It's been a delight. When I reached 49, I know huh - I decided to put down on paper a selection of short stories that I had not conceived yet. Every one of these stories, beginning with a blank slate then filling in the spaces with a tale. By the time I reach my fiftieth year on this incredible planet I could look back and see in black and white (with the cost-of-living crises we are not doing colour anymore) what I had achieved. For some this may not mean much. But for me it's about these small challenges. Did some days I see the blank slate and could not foresee any etchings? Sure. That's what made it a challenge. Then at times ideas emerged uncontrollably, mismatched, chaotic and disjointed determined to find some sort of structure.

And eventually here we are. A year and fifteen short pieces of fiction later. It's a right mixed bag. With many tales with dark stings in their tails and other yarns full of hope and optimism it's a pick n mix (without the lingering saliva from kid's fingers sticking to them).

Thank you to Mr Mark Parsley who gave me the ideas for a couple of them and read the unedited versions with a dose of much appreciated constructive feedback. Mark and his wife, Sharon are the masterminds of the fantastic festival Sharkfest so indeed know their stuff about creating wonderful worlds.

Prey by Ashen Reach (check them out, they are a phenomenon) was the stimulus for the story that shares its title – the longest story of the collection. It's a tale I hope does the song some justice. If not, sorry guys.

All the earnings from this collection goes to charity - so if you have stolen it, go buy it. A big thank you to Ruth who in most cases was glad I was locked in my mancave with it. Your patience is deep. And thank you to all the artists who create. I hear and watch so many bands and their creations are simply wonderful. Art is important. No matter what the politicians will tell you.

So, thank you. Be kind to yourself and each other and hunt down that inspiration. It's all over the place, you just got to grab it.

Big love,

Pete (Not yet 50) K (but very nearly) Mally

2023 (Before May 23rd)

CONTENTS

BEACHED HEN

Eric Cope takes the last two stone steps up from the canal and past the Canal Tavern. As per usual, he glances through the pub's window and sees him sitting at the bar drinking his Guinness. And once again, he quickly looks down at his scuffed boots as they stride along the pavement, then up at the clouds blanketing the sky above continuing his short daily journey to pick up his newspaper.

On his way back, the folded newspaper is under his armpit, sheltered slightly from the light drizzle as he glances through the window and notices Marc still sitting there. Placing his flat cap tighter over his head and with one hand pushing his collar flatter against his neck, Eric takes the familiar walk down the stone steps, back towards the canal to The Beached Hen.

The Beached Hen. The canal boat which undoubtedly was the envy of his friends and the envy of the band. Their envy was deserved, Eric thought. He had saved for it, paid, and cared for it, looked after it as well as anyone did after a home. He had been house proud and proud to be so. Unlocking the door and walking in, boots still firmly on feet, he wondered, not for the

7

first time, why he even bothered these days. A decade ago, his boots, as well as any visitors' would be sitting outside next to the

immaculate and pristine paintwork. Now the faded exterior with the cracked paintwork was probably the most respectable part of the boat. Eric shuffled into the narrow living quarters and

slumped on the armchair placing all the sections of the broadsheet onto the floor. Eric's daily routine was to skim through the paper and begin then from the sports pages. Today was no different.

He pushed the travel segment aside with his boot and wondered how long ago he had

hoovered. He knew the answer. He glanced at the rest of the living area. Many empty bottles lay on and against the dusty cabinet. The rug had changed colour from purple and yellow to grey. Boxes upon boxes had been stacked up, some ripping where the damp seeped into the cardboard. Plastic bags surrounded them, some from supermarkets Eric realised didn't even exist even more. A bike leant against the wall, now more rust than bicycle. He stared at the window, the grey net curtain hanging limp, a spider slowly dissecting a fly caught up in the mesh. The windows would be too filthy to see out of anyway. He turned the page of his newspaper, thought again of Marc sitting at the bar and sighed.

His mind without influence moved from the black and white written word to the

kaleidoscopic loud room of the Canal Tavern twelve years ago. He knew it was twelve years ago, he didn't need to count the seasons. They say time flies. They are wrong.

The Canal Tavern was a hive of noise, a den of fun and of friendships. He remembered the overpowering smell of the air freshener in the men's toilet and the slight tear on the left-hand side of the pool table – compliments of Jax, a cue and too much Bell's whiskey. Every Friday, Bad-Ass

Blues played and every Friday the crowd simply loved them. Eric looked through his own eyes at this different time but the same life. Just. His bass guitar slung over his shoulder, his fingers hitting every note, maybe not perfectly but with enthusiasm, as the singer Paddy rubbed himself up and down the microphone stand like a dog on heat. Eddie playing guitar next to him and Marc hitting these drums like there was no tomorrow. Sweat dripping all round, the stage smelled of sweat, rock, roll and

cheap deodorant. Fun being had and the crowd singing along to every single word.

Every single Friday without fail. The band could have toured, they could have seen more of the country, mingled with more people, got drinks bought for them in new pubs in new cities, slept with more strangers. But they just wanted to play their music in their pub in their home city. They loved it, they loved each other, and the locals loved them for it. On a Friday evening all four members of Bad-Ass Blues hit legendary status. Free drinks, free spirits, and free sex. Life was loud and life was good. Marc and him on the Guinness, Eddie and Paddy on the vodka and cokes. The drinks were known and always stocked up.

He mused on the company he kept at the Beached Head. If one member of the band didn't stay over, Eric always had plenty of young ladies to entertain on the spotless canal boat. Not for the first time in the past twelve years he glanced down at the filthy carpet and wondered when the last

time he had had sex on it. Twelve years, one hundred and forty-four months since anybody apart from him had stepped foot into his home. In that time only his boots had walked into The Hen.

The argument had started in an anger fuelled, alcoholic haze, involving a young lady no doubt, but Eric's memory of it was so blurred. Eric recalled it couldn't have been long after they had finished their set, as their instruments were still on the stage. He remembered angry words between Marc and himself, born out of adrenaline and alcohol. Their voices had got louder and louder as the pub got quieter and quieter. Making a fist and punching Marc as hard as he could in his face was a memory he still vividly recalled. The noise of his nose smashing still lived clearly in his head. Clearer than his sister's graduation or his father's funeral. Replaying this a million times never made it less painful.

Marc falling, the blood flying through the air as he had been dragged out the Canal Tavern by at least two people. He couldn't recall who they were. Remembering the anger still bubbling inside him as he stood outside the pub. The anger did fade and transformed into a feeling of shame. Eric - musician, local hero, well-known and well-loved, had shown everybody the ugly version of him. His head hung and he walked back to the Beached Hen, unusually for a Friday night, alone. He would

apologise to Marc, the pub, the band and to the customers tomorrow. He fell asleep and dreamt of despair.

Twelve years had passed and still no apology. He didn't know if Bad-Ass Blues found a

replacement, or if they were no more. He didn't care. Twelve years. The Beached Hen accumulated twelve years of dust and grime as Eric watched television, read the newspaper and occasionally did sudoku puzzles.

In that time, he had bought a new smartphone and visited his mum in Newcastle twice.

Once due to duty, the other due to her funeral. In these years he had not cleaned, played bass, laughed, or indeed made anybody else laugh. He turned another page and thought of his bass guitar, possibly still sitting in the pub or in a Cash Converters store up in the high street somewhere.

A sigh escaping from his mouth once more, he stood up and placed the newspaper onto the chair.

Leaving the canal boat, Eric walked up the stairs towards the Canal Tavern. He saw Marc was still sitting at the bar.

Twelve years.

Eric felt the pounding of his heart as his palms began to sweat. He tried to get his legs to go through the door of the pub, but they didn't want to.

Gingerly, he opened the door of the Canal Tavern and walked up to the bar and sat at the empty stool next to Marc McNorrie.

Marc turned left and slowly downed what was left of his drink. Eric felt he had a million things to say but no words could be formed. Throat feeling tinderbox dry and stomach clenching. Gripping the side of the chair, Eric watched Marc's eyes flit to him then to his own empty pint glass then to the barman who Eric did not recognise.

"Same again?" Marc said, indicating to his empty glass.

"And one for my friend here."

TECHNICAL CHALLENGE

"Ready… steady …"

"BAKE!"

Giggling, she held her mug of hot chocolate in both hands, the steam diffusing through the air supplying that sweet, wonderful cocoa smell throughout the living room. Angela Langsbirch utterly adored Noel Fielding and Matt Lucas, although she felt Matt had lost a little too much weight for his own good. *He looked ill and less happy. He should be eating more of these showstoppers*; she thought as the cameras focused on the remaining contestants. Pastry week was her favourite, and it was the one she had been looking forward to. She would by no means call herself an expert in the art of pastry making, but she knew the basics and understood the trials and tribulations well enough. As the first sip of the rich chocolate was appreciated, made with full fat milk for that creamy texture, she hoped Abdul would win Star Baker this week. Abdul had been consistent in his bakes and charming and, although this was the quarter final, he had never won Star Baker or ever been given a Paul Hollywood handshake. Shame really, Angela mused with a little hope in her heart.

Leaning back after placing her hot chocolate on a coaster, she straightened a cushion to her left, as Sandro described why he was making Key Lime vol-au-vents to Paul Hollywood and Prue Leith. Angela admired the presenters as well as the contestants. Having Prue on the show was a touch of class. Prue was funny, charming and around the same age as Angela herself. It was frankly delightful for the slightly mature woman to be represented on television. *Maybe,* she mused, *it would be good after all if that Sandro got Star Baker. What a handsome man he was.*

Watching Sandro charm Prue, she wondered when the knock on the front door would come. It *would* come, of that she was sure, but was desperately hoping it wouldn't be before the showstopper. Missing the elimination was one thing but missing the elimination, the showstopper *and* the technical would be simply awful. Especially if Sandro or Abdul won the Star Baker of the week. The glorious creamy liquid chocolate filled her mouth but even the sweet silky texture and the madcap antics of Noel and Matt couldn't fully distract her from thinking of the knock on the door and, subsequently, the situation. Unhappy was an accurate word to describe her, that was certain. The media of late had talked about depression, the menopause (that ship had long sailed), mood swings, anxiety and if Angela was honest with herself, she did not know which one, if any of these, applied to her. But she *did* know that she was unhappy. That was a sure

15

thing. As sure as anything, anyway. And unfortunately, Noel and Matt were only at hand for about ninety minutes per week. They should be prescribed by the NHS.

Her unhappiness stemmed partly because she knew Mick was having an affair. Suspicion had been present for a while, but last week when he had left his phone unlocked and went to the garden to see what the banging was, she had quickly checked his messages.

And since Angela had looked at what code he had entered when he unlocked his phone – 1960 (his year of birth – she had never married him due to his originality) - she had constantly been checking his messages when he was in the shower or taking other business in the bathroom. Hence where he was tonight was exactly known. His location was noted when she was tucked up with a lovely mug of hot chocolate and one of the best television series, *The Great British Bake Off*. It was just a shame it had moved channels and gained adverts.

The dominoes pub team, she also discovered, had not seen Mick for over six weeks. The response was to simply roll her eyes last week when he departed after the early evening news saying "I hope Hoss doesn't cheat tonight, like last week. Bye dear - see you around eleven."

Megan Wilson. Yes, she had thought many times about Megan Wilson.

Megan Wilson. Mrs Wilson (Not Miss or Ms but still Mrs Wilson) the poor widow of Edward Wilson who had missed her dear husband so much she had kept her title and reached out to Mick. Angela was sure poor Megan Wilson had reached out to *many* a man but well, of course Mick would oblige. Poor sad, desperate, needing to be loved Mick.

Attempting to refocus on the television show, now the technical challenge had started her mind went from Mrs Wilson to Mr Fielding.

The technical challenge this week was the constructing, filling and displaying of the spring roll.

Angela approved. She always found herself admiring the ingredients they had been given and, if she was being true to herself, that feeling of admiration often swung to a pang of jealousy. The contestants' ingredients looked fresh and varied. Angela had to be careful what ingredients she used in her everyday cooking and baking, as Mick was allergic to all sorts. White chocolate brought him out in a rash, dried fruit gave him particularly bad wind. Gluten in high doses supplied constipation. Gelatine, ulcers. This list was endless. But the peanut allergy was the worst. That was the big one, the big cheese, public enemy number one. The big NO of the non-negotiable dietary requirements.

As the contestants filled pastries with their delicate fillings, Angela thought back to her weekend shop. Last Sunday in Tesco. That was the easy part. The shop. The difficult part of the plan was waiting until he was in the shower. After searching his trouser pockets, which were splayed carelessly on the bedroom floor she removed his wallet. The temptation to check the messages on his phone was itching at her but she did not scratch, not this time. Time was of the essence. Angela carried his wallet downstairs into the kitchen, removed the condom cases, a look of disgust on her face and, this was the difficult bit – possibly not as tricky as the delicate operation of adding the perfect amount of filling to the spring rolls Paul and Prue were about to inspect, but difficult just the same – injected the peanut oil into each sachet. The syringe was small and fidgety, imagining Prue was standing over he left shoulder smiling and proud, gave Angela more confidence. Although she knew they were not actually present, she wasn't mad after all, she imagined Paul Hollywood's sharp blue eyes bearing down at her as she injected each sachet with just enough of the oil to have an impact, but to not be observed. Thankfully, with Prue, Matt and Noel there she could simply ignore the judging eyes of Paul and carry on. Replacing the condoms in the section of the wallet where they were found, and dropping the small syringes in the bin, she walked back upstairs and placed the wallet back into his trouser pocket just as the bathroom door open sprang open.

Curiosity killed the cat, but the phone would be still checked later if she could.

The hot chocolate was finished and, as the empty mug sat on the table, she watched intently as the contestants sat in a row, holding hands. The dramatic pause. Noel announced the Star Baker. It was neither Sandro nor Abdul but, to Angela's relief, neither of them had been eliminated either, so they would both be going through to the semi-final next week.

That was good, she thought. The semi-final was always exciting. The contestants hugged as there was a heavy knock on the door. Angela stood up, taking the mug into the kitchen en route. Cleanliness was next to godliness. She glimpsed through her blinds from her kitchen window at the police car and the silhouette of two men at the door.

Opening the door, both men looked forlorn as she welcomed them in. *They had bad news to tell her,* their stern exhausted faces told. They sat on the sofa and told her of the untimely death of Mick Langsbirch. Angela hoped she bore the same expression Maxy had when she was told she would not be sharing the semi-final with Abdul, Janusz, Sandro and Syabira.

She really did hope Abdul would win Star Baker next week.

19

PAPER CROWN

I often wonder if it is only my head that Christmas paper hats do not fit. Everyone around the table seems to be able to ignore theirs but mine keeps sliding down and agitating my skin. As another sprout enters my mouth, I wonder if I remove my hat would anybody notice. I swallow the sprout, feeling the need out of politeness to clear my plate. There was so much turkey I feel I am getting the meat sweats although it may be due to the heating being on so high. Gemma must still have poor circulation after all these years. I recall she told me that on one of our first dates nearly twenty years ago now, and hence why she feels the cold.

Taking another sip of my wine, I smile at what is being said. I don't quite make it out but I'm assuming it's a joke from the cracker that Ellie has just pulled with her mum. Gemma had read out the joke, but Ellie got the prize. As my face is hidden by my glass I realise (as I probably do every year and then forget) that she had always let our kids get the prizes from the Christmas crackers. She has that knack of holding them without winning. Maybe it's a mum thing. The tablecloth is full of bowls full of sprouts, potatoes, carrots, peas. The carved turkey proudly in the middle. Scattered around these bowls are several red napkins, shrapnel from the Christmas crackers including a discarded paper hat, a compass, a pencil sharpener some dice and one of these strange fishes which folds when put on your palm. All things I can predict will be placed in a drawer and thrown out unused in about five years' time. A jug of water and two bottles of wine fill the remaining gaps. I notice cranberry sauce stains and a trail of peas going from the bowl to Sammie's plate. He never had got the knack of bringing the bowl to him instead of the other way around.

There are, including me, five of us around the table, with two empty chairs filling the spaces. One opposite me and the other at one of the heads of the table.

I move the warm wine around my mouth, removing some of the dried turkey stuck in between my teeth. The smell of cranberry sauce and the shuffling of chairs soon takes me back – to another year of the same date.

Gemma holding up her hand smiling when the wine was passed around.

"Of course," Eric had said laughing. Gemma had replied by rubbing her belly.

I'm sure it was the same tablecloth and napkins, but I seem to remember the sprouts were more tender and the laughter was a little louder. The second year of our marriage and Sammie yet unnamed and unborn. But well on the path. He had five weeks to go to emerge and be an integral part

22

of the world then. At both ends of the table as usual sat Eric and Margaret – Gemma's mum and dad. Eric sporting his smart blue shirt and knitted jumper over the top of it, even though the heating was cranked up to full, and Margaret laughing loudly at the idea of her daughter being pregnant. "Now you will know what I had to put up with all those years ago," she had said and bellow more contagious laughter. Eric, a small wiry man laughed back, and I remember we laughed for the remainder of the meal.

"Come on," Margaret said, getting up from her seat, unusually elegantly seem to remember for a larger lady, "it's time for Liz."

We moved to the sofa, Eric to his armchair. We took our wine with us, apart from Gemma who brought over the whole bottle of Schloer, and Eric switched on the television. The four of us sat and watched Queen Elizabeth talk about the troops in Iraq and Afghanistan and refer to the past and the anniversary of the televised speech. "To remember what happened 50 years ago means that it is possible to appreciate what has changed in the meantime," she had said, looking deep into the camera. The four of us watched as she stood in her peach dress and gold brooch in front of the large Christmas tree and the window showing a part of the grounds. "It also makes you aware of what has remained constant." As the message ended and a black and white clip of 'God Save the Queen' from the original 1957 broadcast played, I witnessed the pride in both Eric and Margaret's faces.

I think back to that moment. My slightly uncomfortable Christmas jumper pulling tight around my overfull belly, sitting next to my pregnant wife and her parents watching and smiling. The feeling of contentment filling the joyous celebratory living room.

"You want another?" Stephen asks me, removing me from my reflective thoughts.

I look at my empty glass and nod politely. "Go on then."

He leans over, pouring me some more wine; his shirt sleeve I notice dangerously near to the cranberry sauce.

"So, Mark, you still playing?"

I look at him over the table. He manages to dodge the cranberry sauce which I realise I am slightly gutted about as the shirt looks expensive. His thick black hair is receding a little, but I must confess he still looks good for his age, which is a bit older than me. He is clean shaven, and his teeth appear to have been polished with Tippex they are so white. He has an athletic build which does not appear to be waning but with a slight pang of joy I realise the crow's feet around his eyes are entrenched. I steal a glance at Gemma next to him and I realise she has also aged quite a bit in the last few years. I suppose we all have if we choose to acknowledge it. I also now notice she is less reluctant to dye the odd stray grey and her neck is somehow looking more venous.

"A little," I say as I smile back at him. "Same band but don't get out as much as we would like. Still fun though."

"And so it should be," he replies smiling, exposing those white teeth. I am beginning to understand what Gemma sees in him. And in his defence, I concede Ellie and Sammie do seem to like the man. Well, as much as two teenagers like anyone who is now married to their mum and who isn't their dad. And he has never, to my knowledge, stopped me from seeing them or given my children any reason to question my love for them. I have always had my two weeks holiday with them, always had the weekends and special days and Gemma has always insisted I come to their home for the Christmas meal to show, in her words "maturity in front of the children." He has never opposed it. I probably would, to be fair. Or at least try to look at alternatives. Although what happens behind closed doors is a mystery, I am sure he is, as my father used to say, "a good egg."

I suppose people thought Gemma and I were the perfect couple. They, like me, didn't observe the small cracks being neglected and the slight jabs transforming into cutting comments. Glancing at Ellie, still glued to her smartphone like every teenager in the country, I suppose Gemma and I don't do too badly. Sammie is still upstairs on the phone to his girlfriend although I suspect he is playing an online game of some sort, temporarily escaping the family meal which at that age can be painful. I should go up and get him, but Gemma seems calm, and I don't like to overstep my boundaries in what is now her home. As my paper hat slides, I decide I can now remove it without looking like a party-pooper.

"Absolutely," I say. "You okay Eric?"

Eric looks up at me and gently smiles. It's a tired smile that conveys he is okay, and he isn't okay. Eric has always been welcoming of me coming over for the Christmas meal and again I must respect him for that. Even through the divorce Eric and Margaret never pushed me away or sided publicly with their daughter. I can see Eric glancing to the other room where is wife is. Margaret will be sitting there, in front of the spare television in her comfortable chair with a blanket over her lap. Her eyes may be closed or open but either way she will not be that aware of her surroundings and that Christmas Day has come around again. Her now thin body is a shell of the powerhouse she once was. I know Eric insists on as little help as he can. I simply cannot comprehend the effort it takes him to wash, bathe and dress her as well as look after all her needs. He may be small in stature, but I know he is strong. As strong as they come. I could not do it; I am sure of it. I don't think I've ever met a more gentle but proud man in my life.

I miss Gemma's mum's laugh. I hear that sound again echoing through my mind. It may have been the last time I heard it in real life. Ellie was around eight, and Sammie ten years old. I remember because he wouldn't take off his *Ben Ten* t-shirt that year. Even for Christmas Day. The photograph of them both on that day kneeling in front of the tree always makes me smile. It is in pride of place, framed and on my living room wall. I recall us all sitting around the table, Christmas hats on, fidgeting with the toys from the crackers. It didn't matter how much technology was at their disposal, the small plastic objects always dominated during Christmas dinner. Even the bottle opener that never really worked. The same table, the same tablecloth, and the same red serviettes. Rosie, Gemma's younger sister, had returned to the United Kingdom from New Zealand for that Christmas period. It was the only time I ever met her, and she was great company. Her husband had left her for a younger woman and as the divorce proceeded, she had decided to give herself a break and take the trip to visit family and friends. Gemma had warned me, she may be a wreck, so please be tactile. But she wasn't. She was loads and loads of fun. I recognised she shared her sister's nose, her mother's thick hair and her father's sly wit.

27

Sammie and Ellie loved having their aunt come visit and spoiling them rotten with gifts, trips out and unlimited attention. Combined with Eric's gentleness and Margaret's bellowing laugh, it was a simply a wonderful Christmas Day. Thinking back, Margaret had lost weight then, but the vitality was still present, and her laugh was still contagious. It was a joyous time, before financial concerns, unsatisfaction with career progression and slight differences in parental decisions formed a wedge between Gemma and me. I will never forget all sitting around the television, Eric in the armchair, Gemma, Margaret and I on the sofa, Rosie on the ground with the kids all watching Queen Elizabeth talk to the nation. She stood, dignified in a peach dress paying tribute to the survivors of the terrorist attacks that shook our nation and gave her prayers to the Grenfell Tower victims. Reflecting on milestones she spoke of her seventieth wedding anniversary, her husband's decision to step down from duties, William, and Kate's soon to be third child and the engagement of Prince Harry and Meghan Markle.

"Whatever your own experiences this year; wherever and however you are watching, I wish you a peaceful and very happy Christmas." As she concluded, I saw Margaret and Eric's face light up.

"God bless her," Eric muttered taking his hat off and folding it on his lap. As I remember, even the children were quiet during the seven minutes broadcast.

"Where's Sammie? I'll go and get him." Gemma's voice pierces my thoughts now as I shuffle in preparation to stand up.

"Don't worry," Stephen says smiling, "I need to go to the little boys' room anyway."

I watch him stand up, purple hat still firmly on his head. I stupidly wonder if it will still be on when he returns and how it does not seem to be sliding from his head as his forehead seems marginally smaller than mine.

"Thanks babe," Gemma replies as he walks sideways past the chairs and to the doorway. "Can you just put your head round and see if mum needs anything?"

"Of course, dear." And he is out the door checking on poor Margaret.

I look over to Ellie, her fingers exploring buttons on her phone faster than I have ever seen. Occasionally she puts the device upwards and pouts like a duck, doing something very strange with her fingers. I decide not to ask her what she is doing. Firstly, to prevent looking uncool and secondly because in this house currently I don't really know if it's my responsibility. Instead, I say, "So Ellie, you had a good day? Enjoyed yourself?"

She looks up and smiles. Her bright blue eyes and blond hair painfully reminded me of her mum and yet my mum. "Yeah Dad. Thanks. It's been great. And thank you again for all the nice things. Colette's well jealous." She laughs. And so do I. I may not understand the obsession with social media, the return of eighties fashion and the lingo, but I do know she is a good kid.

"Good," I say laughing as Sammie comes into the room, phone also in hand. I can see the resemblance with me now. A thing I never saw when he was younger, especially when people kept on mentioning it.

"Sorry guys," he laughs. "I'm not gonna lie. I was watching Tic Tok and got carried away."

Gemma pulls out his chair and laughs. I am not a hundred percent what he means by Tic Tok but decide to smile also.

Stephen then walks back in and sits in his seat, giving Sammie a rub on the head. My stomach twists a little with jealousy, but Sammie just smiles back. I try to hide my feelings outwardly by covering my mouth with my wine glass.

"Your mum is fine dear."

"Thanks Stephen," Gemma replies.

I slowly stand up, the weight of the food, the slight feel of the wine and the mixed emotions of appreciation, jealousy and perhaps a little regret making me feel both lethargic yet eager to be on my way. "It's been so great to be here," I say, "but I better make tracks. Thanks again everyone."

"Hold on Mark." As he talks, Eric stands. I notice for the first time today he has a slight hunch, and his arms are very thin. "You can't go before the Queen's speech. It's on any second now."

And as I remain standing, he shuffles over to the television set and switches it on. Before he sits down in his armchair, he retrieves the remote control and turns up the volume.

"Just in time," he mumbles and places his arms on the chair rest.

Stephen and Gemma walk over to the sofa and sit down, with Ellie squeezed in next to her mum. Sammie also walks over, phone still in hand and perches on the arm of the sofa. I stand behind Eric's chair and watch as Queen Elizabeth II sits in front of the Christmas tree, sporting a bright red dress and the brooch she wore during her honeymoon.

"Although it's a time of great happiness and good cheer for many, Christmas can be hard for those who have lost loved ones. This year, especially, I understand why."

I look around the room. I see Eric watching as his Queen talks to him, his beloved wife in the next room stuck between one world and the next. I wonder how many times he hears that powerful loud laugh in his mind's eye and wishes he could hear it again in reality. I look down at my two children, happy teenagers who are loved and looked after. Living with their mum and their stepdad and seeing their actual father very regularly.

"I am sure someone somewhere today will remark that Christmas is a time for children. It's an engaging truth, but only half the story. Perhaps it's truer to say that Christmas can speak to the child within us all. Adults, when weighed down with worries, sometimes fail to see the joy in simple things, where children do not."

I glance at Stephen and feel no hate. Jealousy yes, envy yes. Hate – no. He is a good man; I am sure of that. And my eyes swing to Gemma. My wife in a different lifetime. The meals we shared, the laughs we had, the love we developed. All gone. Or is it? Is it just now different? I again look at the large television where Elizabeth is talking to her subjects.

"As the carol says, 'The hopes and fears of all the years are met in thee tonight'" our Queen says as I see Eric smiling reaching high in his face.

"I wish you all a very happy Christmas."

BRAND NEW DAY

The firework display danced gracefully over Sydney's Harbour Bridge and its Opera House as he ate the last bite of the coronation chicken sandwich and burped, staring at the empty plate on the table. Having another one would finish the leftovers in the fridge, but surely starting some new habits today instead of would do no harm? A crumb from the crust remained on his lips and a burp escaped. The empty plate sat on the table. *Not bad*, Andy thought wondering if there really was enough coronation chicken left over in the fridge for another one. With his tea being supped, crumb now dislodged, the decision was that eating another sandwich, chicken left over or not, would not be the best of ideas. If he was going to start fresh tomorrow it would do Andy no harm to get as match fit as possible. Recently reading both *Eat Well, Feel Well* and *Unlimited Energy* he had to admit of late his diet wasn't what it should be. Taking another sip of hot tea, the television showed images of the thousands and thousands of people wet from the recent thunderstorms celebrate the New Year in Australia. The crowds, although very damp, seemed in jubilant spirits which made Andy himself smile as he sat on the sofa, his legs buried below him, a warm indoor hoodie covering his slightly chilly but not uncomfortably cold body. Although the warm tea was certainly making the cold dissipate. Glancing at the ever-present clock on the bottom right of the TV screen, he saw it read 13:02. Andy loved the constant reminder of the time on these 24-hour news channels. Breakfast news was the flavour of choice in the mornings, before work with the clock in the corner of the screen - a constant reminder of the time. Breakfast was usually done between 06.30-06.40, leave the house no later than 6.58 pm. If the 7am headlines could be heard, he was running late for the bus. But in the daytime, when on holiday or a day off, Andy especially loved it. Particularly on such an excitable hopeful day as New Year's Eve. Today, he watched the clock and saw it less as a clock and more of a countdown to the future. His future, where the skin from old life will be shed and new changes will be applied. A metamorphosis if you will. *A bright beautiful butterfly*, he thought, and that smile formed again against the cloud of steam emitting from the mug engulfed in his hands.

With tea finished, even though it may have slightly burnt his mouth Andy stood up from the large settee to return his empty plate to the kitchen. Standing still for a few seconds he looked at the exercise bike. His *brand-new* stationary exercise bike. He imagined there was a new technological snazzy name for it but was happy with simply calling it the exercise-bike.

Sticking a finger to a crumb on the plate and placing it in his mouth Andy smiled again. A lot of that was being done today, he mused. Four hours previously there stood a intimidatingly large cardboard box in the living room, its sides masking-taped up, the instructions boldly along the side informing which way up it was meant to be. Now, in place of the large package stood a new machine that would shed the pounds, make fat disappear and above all make him feel better, physically as well as mentally. Admiring the black finish with the dashes of blue, it seemed to Andy not only high quality but *well*-constructed. Allowing himself a slight nod of pride in his work. "Some people want it to happen, some wish it would happen, others make it happen. Isn't that right Michael Jordan?" Andy said to no-one as he finally went through to the kitchen, placing the plate firmly in the basin. For many, it would have been easy to build, it did come with all the parts, the tools, and a set of instructions after all, but to Andy it certainly wasn't an easy task to construct solo. Yet construct solo is exactly what he did. Two years ago, in fact *last* year he would have probably simply given up, left it unfinished, cleared the cardboard away and felt unsatisfied. But even alone, today the building of the bike had been achieved. It would historically had been a thing that Sandra and he might have worked together on, Andy probably organising the tools and reading the instructions and Sandra placing each component systematically to the next. When things got tricky, the kettle would be filled and switched on whilst she fidgeted and worked out the solution. But she was long gone, that ship had sailed, no teamwork to make the dream work – and he, Andy, the *new* and *improved* Andy Klassman had put it all together – and achieved it completely and utterly on his own. Independently.

Recalling when the seat was screwed in brought another smile to his face - the last section. Testing it was secure and watching Samoa celebrate in their new year, he gave it one more twist, stood back and admired the handy work. After removing all the packaging, the bin for some, the cardboard in the recycling bag, and placing the tools, instructions and paperwork in a bottom drawer in the kitchen, it was tested for a mere ten minutes, sitting and cycling - not as a work-out per say but to ensure the components were in working order. They were. Andy would be on it a lot more starting tomorrow and he certainly didn't want to kick off this new exercise regime on the first day of the new year hunting for a disregarded tool kit. Walking back into the living-room and admiring the handy work again he didn't even attempt to suppress a smile. His face could get used to these muscle movements. It had taken a long time to smile again, and the feel of it on his face felt simply beautiful. At first it had felt alien, but time had gotten him used to the sensation. He had really noticed how much he was grinning earlier when the decision had been made to open the laptop, log on to social media and unfriend more than a hundred people. People whom he had really never met in the real world. Andy was adamant that most of them - if not all of them - would never even notice. Once satisfied, the next step was going through his email accounts, both (Gmail and Yahoo), deleting first the spam, then the read, then the unread messages. Again, highlighting his screen and clicking away, not one company attempting to sell products that were never wanted or needed would be any of the wiser. Over three thousand unread emails gone. Doubting that it would make an emotional difference when he first read about Inbox decluttering, he did it anyway and to the surprise of Andy it felt great. Sitting back down on his sofa, he completed the mental checklist in his head, fingers moving in a swoosh movement as chores were ticked off – washing machine on – check. Exercise bike – check. Email and social media declutter – check. Today, he realised, was what people referred to as one hell of a productive day. Face muscles contracted again, another smile forming on that recently shaved face.

The amount of clothes in the discard pile had both shocked and pleased him. How many t-shirts did he own for God's sake? And why on earth did he even buy that itchy Christmas jumper with the two snowmen with the over exaggerated eyes sharing cocktails with a reindeer again? Two sets of cheap flip-flops sat on top of the pile, like two proud tired mountaineers celebrating their climb. They sat directly on a pair of ripped jeans (not ripped from fashion sense but completely from age sense) and a purple pair of Converse which were torn from the sole to the canvas (again wear and tear rather than a fashion statement.)

Andy briefly recalled when these flip-flops had been worn. August - two years ago. Remembering him and Sandra walking hand in hand through the streets of Benidorm avoiding the drunks. That night they had found a tourist bar that resembled a large ship, got drunk on cocktails and watched two tribute bands and a man who juggled flaming coconuts in a leather catsuit. Maybe not the classiest place they had ever been, but they *had* had a good time. And the pool was nice, he recalled as he threw a fifteen-year-old denim jacket over the holiday-wear pile. It knocked one of the flip-flops of the perch. Ten minutes later, stuffing old clothes into two black high quality bin liners, the thoughts of visits to Benidorm and Prague and Barcelona slowly faded away and he noticed from the television that it was now Bangladesh's turn to celebrate the new year.

"Happy New Year Bangladesh." As the words came from his mouth the clock on the rolling news channel now read 6:01 pm. Lifting both full bags carefully so they wouldn't rip, Andy placed them next to the back door and pulled on his trainers with one finger in between the inside of each shoe and his heel. The shed can happily store them until his next visit to the clothing bank. He was grinning again at the decluttering – a physical and mental exfoliation if you will. He knew, in his heart of hearts, in six or so hours the new year would begin and so would his new future. The pathway to happiness was his to choose and he was damn sure on the right track this time. Feeling drunk with giddiness Andy reminded himself he had not even had an alcoholic drink yet and smiled again. Walking towards the shed, bin liners pulling taught from both his hands, he thought 'soon.'

The BBC News channel continued showing the world celebrating another full tilt of the planet. Another revolution of this 4.5-billion-year-old piece of rock around the 4.6 ball of hydrogen and helium. Andy watched the box as a *Year in Politics* was swifty followed by a programme showing clips to sad melancholy music of the writers, actors, poets, singers, and dancers that had also said goodbye to the ball of rock this year. The programme was surveyed with a mixture of sadness and joy, surprise, and indifference. Some of these people he had never heard of – others, amazed that he had missed their passing. Watching great talents and their achievements was both inspiring yet slightly poignant. The shows titles rolled, and he strode back into the kitchen and opened the cupboards. The smile again dominated his face as a plethora of healthy food stood. Pasta, pasta sauce, vegetables, rice. Not a Pot Noodle, packet of Hob Nobs or a family packet of crisps in sight. It was time to indulge in a glass of a small beverage to welcome in this new year. He knew, just *knew* that it was going to be a good one. No, a wonderful generous wonderful, beautiful year. The defining year of his life in fact, the year that kicks off the hopes and dreams of Mr Andrew Klassman, aged 38 and a quarter. Sandra leaving him had hit him hard. If he was honest with himself, he had found it more difficult than he ever would have imagined. Perhaps it was the combination of Sandra moving out to live with an IT consultant called Hamish and the death of Zamo, his beautiful young Staffordshire terrier that pushed down his mood and kept it smothered. At only five years old, Zamo had developed a tumour, not six weeks after Sandra had cleared out her belongings. It was tough. Tough as hell. His mood had darkened and sometimes he thought it would never get brighter. But finally, these two life-changing moments had been accepted and throughout December Andy had decided to move forward and stop wallowing in the past - which undeniably he had been doing for the past three months.

Opening the fridge, he then opened a bottle of Cava and placed it on the worktop. His drinking was also due a reduction, that was one of the many resolutions for the up-and-coming year. Apart from the odd special occasion, alcohol would not be consumed at home. Obviously, once in a while a glass of wine or the occasional pint when he was back dating would be enjoyed. And that he also knew, was on the cards. At first when the thought had occurred, dread had slowly turned to fear. Fear then to nervousness. Now, the mixture of nerves and excitement swilled in his body like a tumble dryer. The initial reluctance to join internet dating sites was now gone and a few carefully chosen ones would go live next week. *A new year, a new more confident me,* he thought as he opened the bottle. Just before grabbing a glass, he looked back into the living room through the open door, the television now showing the celebrations of Germany and Spain. A split screen showing two sets of fireworks in two different countries. Madrid and Berlin both appearing joyful and colourful to Andy as he went back into the kitchen to pour himself the drink.

The last fifty minutes to Andy had flown and his third small glass sat on the table, next to an empty small packet of crisps and a tangerine peel. Jools Holland was delivering his smorgasbord of talent as usual, celebrity crowds sitting in the audience laughing and having fun as the large clock in the television studio wound downwards to midnight. There was ten minutes to go, Andy thought – looking forward to the new year. *Chapter one of The Exciting Life of Andy.* He recalled a quote and said it out loud, "More than ready for the next chapter in my life!"

Only five minutes before, he had picked up his mobile phone, logging onto the holiday website to confirm what he had booked only yesterday. Very pleased that the details still came up, confirming the purchase. Missing out

by not confirming a question or ticking a box would indeed suck but he

had been thorough. Two years ago, the thought of getting onto an

aeroplane and being alone abroad would have set off some form of anxiety

attack but now the feeling was joyful anticipation - greatly looking forward

to the adventure, he could barely wait. The thought of exploring,

discovering historical monuments, meeting new people, and drinking

cocktails in the sun filled his heart with hope and joy. Rome in May and

the big one, New York in August. He could hardly fathom it. Once the

credit cards were in and the initial deposit was paid, the feeling of worry

was immediately exchanged for the sensation of eagerness. The thought of

visiting the Colosseum, the Sistine Chapel, the Empire State Building,

Little Italy, looking at the Statue of Liberty, staring at her like he had done

on many a movie - increased the size of the already wide smile as Jools

Holland continued to interact with his star-studded audience. Andy's new

job was starting in March also – he had checked and double-checked his

holidays with them, absolutely no problem there – and again the

anticipation of that was simply huge. A brand-new career. But more

importantly, he was bizarrely excited for the daily commute. An easy

fifteen minutes by train, working in an office full of hopeful young,

dedicated individuals. During the interview whilst answering the questions as best as he could (obviously, he considered, as they gave him the position, he must have done an outstanding job with these answers) he had become aware of the large office next to the interview room. The large glass walls gave a true insight of what the job would entail if he were successful. As each question was answered as professionally as possible, Andy occasionally looked through the glass wall. Twenty of so staff were sitting at their computers and all smiling, talking to each other, and laughing together. It was the kind of environment that Andy would thrive in, he just knew it. And even meet someone? Someone special or in fact just a good friend. Or even both. Thinking of the possibility he smiled again. It did not matter which one. It would be a place he wanted to go to every day and that was what mattered. It was only two short months away, he thought as he prepared himself for the clock to strike midnight. It was going to be *his* year. Yes Sir, it was indeed. A new job, holidays booked and planned, a new fitness regime and he had even renewed his half-season ticket for The Blades for this season and pre-purchased next season's season ticket at a value price. Absolutely nothing was going to stop Andy live the life of which he had always dreamt. The clock worked itself towards twelve and he felt he was in a Bon Jovi song he was so energised. Picking up the glass of Cava he raised it in the air, getting ready to celebrate the new year. The past was the past, and it was time for action.

The clock arm hit twelve, it chimed, and Jools Holland wished everyone a happy new year, the guests all stood up, raised their glasses and Andy took a large sip of his drink.

"Happy new year," he said. "Here is to the best year ever. Here is to you 2020." His smile did not fade until he found sleep.

THE CALL

It feels like I have not been asleep for long when the phone rings. I slide out of bed ungraciously, the small of my back pulling taut as I stand unsteadily on my feet and walk towards the mantelpiece where the horrendous electronic device is vibrating. My Achilles tendon feels tight and the back of my feet needs a rub but it's not worth the effort or pain it will cause by bending over. The name on the small screen tells me who I already know it is.

Years ago, she had insisted I had put in her number in the phone. After a little hesitation she had taken my phone from my hand, called me from hers and typed in something on mine. I remember her calling me again to show me that her name would come up every time she called. I press the green button and pick up the phone.

"Hello Liz. It's been a while."

"Hello Clive," she replies. It's been five years, since the last time we had talked, when she gave me back my mobile phone which we both knew I didn't really want. Five long years, yet to me nothing had changed in her voice. I pick up the husky tones, the slight Manchester accent. The undercurrent of anxiety I find is still very much present.

"Sorry it's late. Were you sleeping?"

I glance behind at my dishevelled single bed. The bedroom I realise looks just like the living room if someone had teleported a bed into the middle of it. At the age of seventy-four do you still refer to it as a bedroom? Unopened boxes still sit on the floor with a few plastic bags to their side. I notice for the first time in weeks, perhaps months, that dust hangs from the corners of the room and a broken old trestle table is leaning against the wall. I wonder what my house smells of. I mean to a stranger. Would someone who isn't nose blind like me smell the mould? Or the dirt? Or sense the loneliness? I then notice a previously unobserved spider web has formed over the net curtain as it hangs insecurely from the curtain rail. I think about dusting it after the phone call. But I won't. I know I won't. It doesn't matter, it's not as if I get visitors anyway. And spiders eat insects, right? As I move the phone to my slightly better ear, I remember I had promised to keep this mobile phone charged up, for this very moment. As if Liz could read my mind, even from hundreds of miles away she says, "I'm pleased your phone was on, Clive."

I rub my hands over my stubbly face, feeling the callouses against my lip and take a deep breath. "No, it's okay. So, what news? " I ask. Even after all these years it is difficult to hear that voice. The voice I once loved, the voice that sang silly songs to me, the voice that made me laugh louder and longer than anybody else had. I close my eyes and hold them tight for a few seconds longer than necessary. I don't think I could laugh anymore. I think I don't know how.

Laughing. A different life ago. I open my eyes as my back gives me another twitch. I wince at the immediate pain and the knowledge that no matter how many times the planet has orbited the sun the fact that Liz's voice and beautiful face was partially responsible for what had happened pulls at me. Responsible for the son we had made together, the son that we held and fed and loved. We adored that boy. Well as much as we could. We had known he wasn't like the other babies. Of course we knew that, we weren't fools. Or maybe we were. In my heart I knew we had both tried to love and care for him like the other parents did with theirs, perhaps even more so. But that was fifty long years ago.

"Scott." Liz spoke quieter this time.

Fifty years of pain. Fifty years of humiliation. It didn't settle even when Scott had left the relentless public gaze and the spotlight of the national press. The reprimanding glares of the neighbours still lingered. Even when we separated because we couldn't stand to look at each other as we reminded one another what we had brought into this world.

Even after we had hidden from society, after all this time, I thought, I still hate my son's name.

"What about him?" I ask, rubbing the back of my neck now with the tips of my fingers, digging in the flesh with as much force as possible. I open my eyes slowly.

"He's out. They've released him," she said, "he's out."

I close my eyes again, as tight as I can. I never want to open them again. I feel the tears forming as I hold the phone up to my forehead and bow my head in despair.

TO HOLD IS TO HAVE

Downing the remainder of her glass of Prosecco, Jack once again looked at her finger where her wedding ring used to be. He estimated it had been absent for two to three months considering the slight difference in skin tone.

She placed the glass on the polished wooden oversized table. "Back to mine then?"

As these words registered, Jack observed that one eyebrow slightly arched upwards as one side of her mouth ever so slightly did the same, a small action yet to Jack, very much noticed. He assumed that facial expression had hooked, line and sunk many a heart.

"Sounds great." Attempting to act as casual as he could but realising that his voice had risen an octave or two, he tried to cover it by grabbing his jacket from over his chair and placing it over his Ted Smith shirt – which clung on tightly to his muscular physique for dear life. As he placed the jacket over his shoulders, he noticed that Katie Johnson's pupils opened a little wider as she observed the buttons straining to hold over his muscular chest. He tried to stop himself from smiling. If you've got it, flaunt it, right? he thought. He casually tensed his pectoral muscles hoping she would catch their slight movement.

Jack had no idea how much the taxi had cost. Nor did he care. He placed his contactless card on the chip n' pin device, waited for the beep-beep noise, wished the cab driver a pleasant evening and stepped out into the cool late evening air with Katie right behind him. As the automatic door clicked back into place, the taxi sped off. He watched as Katie opened her designer handbag, leant in and grabbed what appeared to be a car fob but thinner and white. Observing her thin delicate fingers press a small button, he was soon aware of electronic private gates in front of them stir into life and slowly open. Looking at the large house now visible to him, impressed not so much by the size but by the modern design, he took Katie's hand gently, gate fob still in her palm and stroked her palm gently with his fingertips.

Heart pounding with the anticipation of what was to shortly come, the cold night air brushed past his face, breaking through his thin flimsy shirt. As he tried to calm his racing heart, he watched her place the gate fob back into her bag and in one slick motion bring out a set of house keys. Observing that even her set of keys, with a simple key ring and two small keys, were delicate. He was slightly mesmerised by her bright red fingernails as the key slid into the keyhole. She turned to him, that slight eyebrow and mouth raise again in perfect synchronicity. This time he couldn't stop himself from smiling back.

As he sat on the unnecessarily uncomfortable but no doubt expensive settee he wondered if he should remove his shoes. Would it look too presumptuous? Overkeen? Perhaps it did - but he *had* been invited back to her place had he not? They both *knew* what was about to happen, surely? He heard the clink-clink of ice cubes from the kitchen, a tinkling over the sound of the chart music that she has put on. The song was vaguely familiar to him. As the singer sang about his ladies and cars Jack decided he should keep his shoes on – at least for the meantime. I mean, he thought he didn't want to mess *this* up. And furthermore, he was not wearing socks. Do people still wear socks? he thought as his mind swiped back to the immediate present, and he smiled as it dawned on him where he was. The glamorous, beautiful and all too sexy Katie Johnson's home. The focus of many an implicit thought of men in and around the Banstead area. Her long blond hair, short skirts, sexy physique, and gorgeous open smile made everyone look twice when she walked past Café Nero or the training ground. He simply couldn't believe he was here. He couldn't help the smile take over his face. He had never been so grateful for having applied his Dolce and Gabbana Velvet Desert Eau De Parfum earlier.

Katie Johnson. The widow of the late, great Johnny Johnson. As Jack heard the fridge door close from the kitchen, he looked up at the framed picture of Johnny on the light purple painted wall. The picture showed him topless holding a large fish. A fair amount of muscle, yes, but covered in a heavy layer of fat. A sure sign of indulgence. Jack considered if he was that great after all. His memory touched on the conversations he had overheard once. Johnny had lost a game and when out of the public gaze he had apparently also lost his temper. This may have been idle gossip but, as Jack well knew, shit sticks in the world of sport and the rumour mill was in full throttle. This indeed wasn't the first of these whispers. "Quick with his feet, quick with his hands." He had heard someone once say over an after-match curry. A premiership league football star, fifteen caps for his national team, five England goals and many more assists. The late great Johnny Johnson was without doubt a world-class player. Yes, Jack thought as he looked up at the fish in his hands, world class but possibly not that great, but then again without any doubt - late. This thought increased his smile so much he had to consciously reduce it as he heard the kitchen light switch off, so Katie wouldn't think him a simpleton. Jack thought back to the press invasion, the funeral, the news bulletins. Two years ago now. How Johnny's wife was still single after two long years he simply did not understand. But tonight, as she stepped back into the room, a glass of gin and tonic in each hand, her skirt tight against her thighs and her vest top clinging to her muscular body, he was certainly not complaining about that little fact. No, Sir.

Not three hours ago, they were both at the large, polished counter at the modern bar with the neon lights, coincidently at the same time. They had exchanged a few polite words. Jack of course recognised her straight away and asked her how she was getting on with her clothing boutique. As she told him that she enjoyed it and enjoyed talking to the customers particularly about the ins and outs of their lives, he caught that eyebrow/mouth lift when she glanced down at his muscular chest. It was just a quick glance, but he was sure, it was most definitely there. She in turn asked him about his football coaching, asking how the kids were getting on as it must be tough with their disadvantaged backgrounds. He was pleasantly surprised that she had known that about him and told her so. They both ordered their drinks for their collective groups and went their separate ways to each side of the bar. Somehow, an hour later they had found themselves back at the bar, their consecutive round again but this time they ordered their parties drinks, delivered them, made their half-baked apologies to their friends, and went straight back to the polished counter forming a party of two.

Watching her intently, she placed a glass into his hand and sat down next to him on the expensive but uncomfortable sofa. Again, he couldn't quite believe he had found himself here. His legs brushed at her bare leg; their eyes locked together. He felt her flesh through his skinny-fit trousers. He saw the raised eyebrow and mouth and this time he leaned in for the kiss.

The sound of the glass smashing was deafening. Jack had never heard a gun fire, but he assumed it sounded a lot like that. As a shard of glass landed on his lap, he pushed away from Katie un-ceremonially. His leg was still touching one of hers as he had been caressing her soft back inches away from her bra clasp. Jack had been working his way slowly but steadily on the way to his destination just as her hand was leisurely but surely working way up his toned thigh. He was enjoying her touch even over his jeans when the glass smashed into smithereens. Some gin sprayed from the exploding glass over one of his cheeks. His first thought was that he had nudged the glass with his foot – he *knew* he should have removed his slip-on shoes – but he soon realised that it wouldn't have made the glass explode *outwards*.

"Oh shit, sorry about that." Katie said wiping her face, "that damn dishwasher is making the glass weaker." She stood up quickly, her skirt to Jack's disappointment falling back down to cover her thigh. Glancing again at the now wet table and the splattering of glass debris he saw something pass over her face. Jack couldn't be sure what exactly. Maybe the glass was a family heirloom. Or extraordinarily expensive. Or had it been frustration, perhaps? But then it was gone. The slight look of anger or surprise or shock or frustration had left. Possibly the alcohol and his hormones were playing tricks with his mind, he thought as he wondered how many seconds he was away from the bra-strap.

"I'll get a cloth," she said and immediately went into the kitchen leaving Jack standing, shaking off a couple of glass fragments from his body, whilst realising the ever-growing lump in his jeans in his crotch vicinity was getting larger. He was still on his feet as Katie returned and as he looked down, he saw that upturned smile and eyebrow again. This time there was no mistaking the meaning. "Oh, forget the cloth", she said smiling, "we can clear it up in the morning. Where were we again? Oh yeah", she took his hand and smiled, "let's go upstairs."

*

As he lay naked, staring at the ceiling where the moon was supplying a teasing of light, the beautiful body alongside his, he felt that sense of cold that he had felt when they first made love. Or at least attempted to. "Don't worry," she had said softly in his ear, "it happens."

To Jack's surprise, she leant over and held him tight in her arms. Not sexually but protectively he realised, perhaps, he mused, like a shield more than a lover. "It happens," she whispered again. But it did *not* happen, Jack thought. Not to him anyway. Yes, he had heard stress, or a bad diet or age can do that to a man. He had seen the adverts on the television and the phone-ins on TV shows. But this was somehow different. Crazy as it sounded, he felt he was being watched, being judged even. The feeling of scrutiny somehow overcame the feeling of lust. He tried to will himself to be the lover he knew he could be. This situation itself should be a fantasy he would keep In storage in future times of despair. It should. But it just felt... Jack stared up at the ceiling he grasped for the correct word. It just felt ....*wrong*. His mind drifted back to that Sunday, many moons ago, a fortnight after his twelfth birthday when the scout watched his every move on the football field. He had messed it up then just as he had messed it up now. He had tried nibbling Katie's ear, feeling her smooth muscular back under his fingers but the sensation of being observed and monitored was still there. Eventually he gave up and stayed - held tightly in her arms. His heart was not the only thing deflated with his failure to perform. Unless she was a class actress, he also realised that Katie did not seem to be that bothered. If anything, he thought she seemed sympathetic. Jack closed his eyes and hoped that he would wake up in an hour or so with a new zest for life so he could make love to this magnificent woman lying next to him. He was a young red-blooded man after all.

He finished his pee, shook himself clean and flushed the toilet ensuring he had not sprayed along the rose gold coloured toilet ring. He was stark naked, goosebumps crawling across his skin although it was an exceptionally warm humid night. He shuffled to the basin, pouring water into his hands and splashing it onto his face, hoping to energise the parts of his body that needed the boost. He simply couldn't understand the lack of performance. He saw a sky-blue cotton towel folded up over the radiator, leaned down and wiped his face on the soft fluffy material. Returning to the bedroom he glanced into the mirror which hung above the sink. He froze. Paralysis overtook him. His feet nailed to the floor; his bones as heavy as steel. Standing still he continued to stare into the mirror. Facing him was a tanned man, one which he recognised from somewhere, somewhen. The man's jowls wobbled, and Jack noticed his hair was dyed so black it actually appeared blue. He was smiling with his mouth. But not his eyes which pierced through the glass. Teeth, obvious veneers as they appeared as white as Tippex and straight as any American superstar. Jack continued to stare, his bare feet still unable to even shuffle, his mouth dropped open like a guppy fish. The smile of the man widened and formed into a laugh. Jack unfroze, his feet finally feeling free, and turned around wondering if Katie could hear the sinister noise. Two seconds later he forced another look. Turning back around again, he saw his own face, the dishevelled hair, the stubble, the tired blue eyes. The face of him. He was looking at himself. No expensive aftershave, no hair products, no wrinkle concealer. Just him. Of course he was. It was a damn mirror for goodness' sake. Nevertheless he reached out his finger and touched it just to make sure, as the finger pressed against the solid glass he felt ridiculous. It squeaked a little just to prove its point and confirm his stupidity. Jack's goosebumps shrouded his body as he shook his head and stepped into the hallway, quietly padding back to the bed, hoping he would see his disregarded boxers-shorts so at least he could cover his failing member, providing the minimum at least of some comfort.

He leant over to reach his phone. It read 04:56 am. He turned his head to see if the light hadn't disturbed Katie, but it didn't appear to have. Jack lay, staring at the ceiling once again. Sweat now emitting from his pores and rolling down his chest, he could feel it pour down his thighs, down the crack of his arse. Cold then hot, hot then cold. Had Covid-19 eventually caught up with him? Fever-like symptoms, yes. Hallucinations and erection failures, no. Not that he knew of anyway. But maybe the news didn't mention that little nugget. Awareness of Katie Johnston, ten years his elder, a hundred times more beautiful than anyone he had ever been with, snoring gently next to him. Sweat ran into his eyes as he closed them shut even tighter. Watching through the slit in the curtain the shadows moved as the moon played its cloud dance. As he lay still, he eventually heard the first bird song. To Jack it did not feel like a song at all. A call or a warning perhaps. But not a song. A wood pigeon made its presence known, its familiar coo-coo greeting the morning. Jack knew that above all he just wanted to get up, changed back into yesterday's clothes and out of this place. His bones ached, his head felt like fuzz, even his teeth seemed to ache. The curtains twitched a little even though the room held no breath, floorboards creaked and beyond his headache he was sure he could still hear laughing coming from the bathroom mirror.

He lay on his back as still as he could and awaited the further rise of the sun. It seemed like forever.

Eventually the star rose high enough in the sky to bathe the room with light and Katie stirred. "I need to go lovely", he said as gently as he could muster and gave Katie a tender kiss on the cheek.

Recovering his jacket from the settee, and pulling it over him a shard of glass fell from it and landed on the carpet.

"Right," he said, as upbeat as he could to Katie who was standing behind him, "sorry for the early start but got to get off. Will Facebook messenger you, though."

"Absolutely," she replied, pulling her dressing robe a little tighter, "thanks again."

"And listen, sorry for..."

"No need to apologise Jack. Talk soon," she said as she walked him to the front door. They both knew they would not.

"Yup," he said as he glanced a look backwards and walked towards the gate which opened as he approached it. He watched her smile, keeping a hold of the white fob in the palm of her hand as the sun beat down on her. The front door soon closed.

Katie placed the fob onto the chest of drawers which sat in the hallway and walked towards the living room, slumping herself on the expensive settee. She looked at the cloth on the table and the shards of glass which remained there sitting in a stain the shape of Europe. She slowly glanced up at the picture of her husband, fish in hands, his blue eyes looking ever proud of himself.

Rolling her eyes, she leant over and grabbed the remote control and drowned out the noise of her own thoughts. "God damn you Johnny", she said as she put her head in her hands. "You possessive bastard. Why can't you just let me go?"

Tears rolled down her face as she watched morning television.

PLATFORM 5

"A medium latte with skimmed milk and a hazelnut shot please."

Max put his hands in his jacket pockets and smiled as he waited at the collection counter, sneaking a sideways glance at one of the most beautiful women he had ever seen. Today she was sporting a pair of bright dungarees, her hair tied up exposing the intricate colourful tattoo on her neck.

She finished zapping her debit card on the small paying machine at the service counter then moved slightly to her left, away from the order queue and hence closer to him just as he was handed _his_ medium latte with skimmed milk and a hazelnut shot.

"Thank you." He smiled as he removed his hands from his pockets, took the take-away cup from the small cheerful barista, smiled briefly again at the woman sporting the dungarees and walked down to the end of the concourse. Platform five was always a busy one. He held his coffee firmly in his hand, feeling his heart racing a little more than before his purchase, as the steam attempted to escape from the small flap in the lid. He knew it wasn't the anticipation of the caffeine hit that had his heart racing. *She* had acknowledged *him*. The beautiful woman at the concourse had acknowledged *him*. He wouldn't bet on it, but he was fairly sure she had shared a smile back at him. Or possibly he was just being hopeful. What did it matter – the beautiful woman with the dungarees had acknowledged his existence and for that he was grateful.

Monday 16ᵗʰ March

"A medium latte with skimmed milk and a hazelnut shot please."

Max again stole a glance. The dungarees were replaced by loose-fitting black trousers, white trainers sticking out of the baggy legs, a light-coloured shirt with a blue denim jacket covering her shoulders. Her hair was down and loose, black wavy hair hanging down the top of her back. This time he dared an early smile as he received his drink from the barista. "Thank you," he said to her then with a quick glance to the woman said, "I need this."

She smiled back at him, her mouth wide, her teeth large and white. He caught the lines forming around her eyes when she did so, and his heart raced. "Me too."

Max walked from the concourse to platform five, the unforced smile stretching his face. She had both smiled and spoken to him. Her smile was in his mind, and he hoped it would stay there all day. He was sure it would. Today, he decided, was going to be a good day. Monday or not. He was already looking forward to the commute again tomorrow.

Tuesday 17. March

Max sat on his sofa, remote control on the arm of the chair, feet up and tucked behind him as he watched the television. A newsreader was reporting on the current situation, but Max's mind could not stray from the girl from the train station. He wondered if Clapham Junction had ever seen such a beauty. As the newsreader passed on to a reporter outside Downing Street, he fantasised about sitting on a train with her, sharing a joke. He thought of holding her hand and laughing alongside her. He pictured himself playing his guitar in his band, but not for the usual crowd of twenty or thirty but for thousands, the dungaree lady from the station in the front row screaming his name. Pride in her eyes. For the past three weeks they had stood on the same concourse in the same train station in the same city and ordered the exact same drinks at the same time. Max didn't necessarily believe in omens but surely this must be a sign.

He wasn't particularly looking for love since he had split up from Emma. In fact, he had made an active decision to be on his own for a while, learn to enjoy his own company and focus on his guitar playing and song writing. With great work colleagues, friends, band members and the occasional family member to socialise with, he certainly wasn't lonely, and he knew he didn't need a partner at this moment in time. Although he was getting used to the idea of singledom, the thought of knowing the woman from the train station with the tattoo and the dungarees better brought a smile to his face more than any band performance could ever do.

Friday 21ˢᵗ March

"A medium latte with skimmed milk and a hazelnut shot please."

His heart was racing, and his throat felt as dry as gravel. He had rehearsed and rehearsed this moment on the walk to the station, not caring if anybody heard him. If only he rehearsed this much for his guitar playing, he thought and tried to smile but the nerves had taken hold. But the moment had come, and he knew he had to take it. He looked over to her, she had dungarees on again but this time a slight faded purple tone, her hair tied up again, tattoo showing. He noticed a pair of high platform black trainers that complimented the outfit perfectly.

"Thank you," he said smiling as he took his coffee from the barista, took a breath, turned around and prepared himself for his planned words. "All the best people drink this."

Everything stopped. Nothing happened for a split second apart from the blood rushing to his head. Then all went silent. Did he really say such a ridiculous thing? In fact, did he say it at all? Out loud? His mind reached out for an answer and then the world went back to normal, the hustle and bustle of the concourse, the noise of announcements and whistles, the smells of coffee, the slight breeze as trains sped by. She smiled back at him, that large open smile immediately lifting him from his doubt.

"Absolutely they do." Her bright teeth captivated him and as he saw her ponytail flick a little, he began to breathe. "Have a good day."

"You too," he said, aware that his smile may result in him looking slightly demented. Holding his hot drink, he walked towards platform five. He felt like he was floating, the air below his training shoes pushing him up and moving him along the platform. What was that accent of hers? Newcastle or Middlesborough perhaps? He allowed himself to wonder if she may be having the same thoughts. He felt ten feet tall and eager to continue the conversation every morning of next week. It was going to be a long weekend.

Monday. 23ʳᵈ March

"Good evening,

The coronavirus is the biggest threat this country has faced for decades –

and this country is not alone. All over the world we are seeing the

devastating impact of this invisible killer. And so tonight I want to update

you on the latest steps we are taking to fight the disease and what you can

do to help.

And I want to begin by reminding you why the UK has been taking the

approach that we have.

Without a huge national effort to halt the growth of this virus, there will

come a moment when no health service in the world could possibly cope;

because there won't be enough ventilators, enough intensive care beds,

enough doctors, and nurses.

And as we have seen elsewhere, in other countries that also have fantastic

health care systems, that is the moment of real danger.

To put it simply, if too many people become seriously unwell at one time,

the NHS will be unable to handle it - meaning more people are likely to

die, not just from coronavirus but from other illnesses as well.

So, it's vital to slow the spread of the disease.

Because that is the way we reduce the number of people needing hospital treatment at any one time, so we can protect the NHS's ability to cope - and save more lives.

And that's why we have been asking people to stay at home during this pandemic.

And though huge numbers are complying - and I thank you all - the time has now come for us all to do more.

From this evening I must give the British people a very simple instruction - you must stay at home."

<u>Monday 15 June</u>

Max stood, the sun beating down on him, his mask covering the lower half of his face. He could feel his breath attempt to diffuse through the cloth, but he somehow couldn't remove the after taste of his toast and butter. Clapham Junction felt strange, alien in fact. He looked up, as people attempted to keep their distance from each other. A busy bustling train station transformed to a hostile clinical area due to something that was first transmitted thousands and thousands of miles away. To Max, it felt everyone blamed each other, people sharply looking in the direction of where they heard coughs, everyday people shaking their heads when their personal space was reduced. It was slightly post-apocalyptic, and he did

69

not like it. Not one bit. He reached the coffee shop but as expected the shutters were still down. It appeared to him the shutters would forever be down. There was no sign of life at the kiosk, just some extra bird droppings on the counter. He dropped his head, adjusted his bag strap from around his shoulders and as his mask tugged slightly from behind his ears, he walked slowly to platform five.

Wednesday 17 June

Max wondered if there were more people in Clapham Junction than yesterday but couldn't quite decide. He did realise that the atmosphere was the same. The quiet hostile unfriendly nature of masked people attempting to keep their distance and panicking when they couldn't. He missed his band more than he would imagine. He missed his friends and his family but at least he had *Zoom* for that. Band practice, in his opinion anyway, needed to be live and organic and that just couldn't be done over a laptop. He had attempted to enjoy his own company, but lockdown had shown him that he tolerated it at a push. He missed people, plain and simple. It was the first day back at work in the office yesterday and he thought it would be great to reconnect but due to the policy of 'bubbles' it felt even lonelier than home. Twenty-five people in an office where the communication was through *Zoom*. The odd nod of the head or the raised voice across a room. No sport to talk about, no gossip over the coffee machine, no lunch time laughter. He reached the coffee shop at the concourse which was still closed and continued to walk to platform five, feeling a sense of emptiness and sorrow. He wondered if the rest of the commuters felt the same.

Friday 19 June

He stood on platform five and sighed. He had some chewing gum in his pocket but the effort of having to lift the mask, put it in his mouth then attach it again changed his mind for him. It wasn't so much the effort but the unnecessary guilt he felt of removing it, even for a second. It was ridiculous he knew that, but the last thing he needed was the silent disapproving looks of a fellow commuter. He thought about the band. Was it disbanding? Possibly. Stephen hadn't commented on the *WhatsApp* group for over a week and Mikey had not mentioned any new song ideas on social media for a while. His mind set about thinking of another day in the office, glancing at his work colleagues from a distance, eating his poorly made packed lunch at his desk whilst scrolling the news on his computer. He thought about his mum, her health not great at the best of times. Would her shoulder operation be cancelled now? Would she be forgotten about? Would she be one of the many statistics plastered on the news every day? He was aware of some slight movement to his left and thought to move to respect the two-metre distance rule that had been pasted all over every visible surface. He glanced at the person's feet near him in

71

case they were unaware of the rules. He recalled the black trainers with the big heels. His gaze rose as he noted the hair, tied up again. Her eyes were blue. Below them, her colourful mask hid that smile, but Max knew how lovely that mouth was even though it was covered. She was holding out two travel mugs, both silver in colour. He looked into her eyes and those smiling lines were present. His mouth under his mask copied the movement.

"Latte with skimmed milk and a hazelnut shot?" she said, and handed him one of the travel mugs.

THE ART OF PERFECTION

The sun was beating down, its warm rays blanketing John Webb, filling him with unadulterated contentment. Life to John was looking good indeed. Ramblin' Man Festival had finally got underway, and the sun was indeed playing its part on this field of music lovers.

John supped his pint of real ale from the plastic pint glass whilst sitting on a wooden bench, opposite the table from his three mates. He took another sip and glazed at the haystack next to him. "Yup, this is the life," he said quietly as he realised he truly felt great. Summer had indeed arrived.

Webby said he felt obliged to go and check out the Rising Stage or even the Main Stage. On his way to his ultimate destination, the wonderful Prog Stage. The Rising Stage was great for the bands who were up and coming, but to Webby it was that same old classic rock, a few verses, a punchy chorus, and an unnecessary and clumsy guitar solo towards the end of each song. The main stage was much of the same. That wasn't to say Webby didn't enjoy it, and he shouldn't go and make the effort, but maybe it was the heat of the sun that was putting him off. Or more likely he was so content with sitting here he simply couldn't be at all bothered.

With seven straight As in his GCSEs, 3 As and 1 B in his A-levels and a First class degree in engineering, Webby knew he was intelligent. He often wondered why people would opt for the camping, and hence put up with the lack of showers and space, when they could just focus a little more and get a Firebird Deluxe campervan like his. That's exactly why he liked playing in his band The Tortoise And The Yellow - their musicianship was second to none. John Webster was proud of his song writing and the rest of the band understood the art of musicality perfectly. It was a hard and precise graft in rehearsals, but the result never failed. Their first E.P was described in a Prog Rock magazine review as 'harmonised perfection', especially their fourteen-minute piece de resistance *Of The Way Of The Path Of the Hammer.*

Just under a week ago, over an americano after rehearsals, Bobby the bass player had been telling Webby that there was no such thing as a perfect performance.

"Zepplin in Earls Court in 1969, Hendrix at Woodstock, Queen at Live Aid were great - but not perfect. These performances are only considered so good nowadays because of the death of the musicians involved. Just like there is no such thing as a perfect job or a perfect crime," he continued as he took a sip of his coffee, "You see in every job you still have one more thing to do to complete it, no matter how small. It's like with a crime. With continual global satellites and modern DNA testing you are never going to get away with a major crime."

"You will see perfection on Saturday Bobby, trust me," Webby replied, took another sip of his coffee and laughed. Bobby laughed with him.

And now Saturday had finally arrived along with the sun, and Webby found himself sitting on the bench with Bobby, Marcus his guitarist and Toby the keyboard player. Sam had said he may try to make an appearance but his in-laws were "poorly" so their drummer would have to "play it by ear."

"Fancy a trip to the Prog Stage guys? *Left-Hand Orcs* are starting off soon. Danish, I think?" Marcus asked, squinting in the Kent sunshine.

"Yeah, we'll finish these and grab some more and then head over. That good with you guys?"

"Perfect Webby", Marcus replied, finishing the last of his drink and placing the plastic pint glass on the table.

Bobby also placed his empty pint container on the table and wiped his mouth with the back of his hand.

Webby stood up, grabbed all three of the empty reusable cups and walked to the bar which was in a tent that smelt deeply of grass and hops. He soon returned with four more drinks in one of those specifically designed cardboard containers that resembled large egg boxes, and placed it on the table. As everyone removed their pint Webby said, "Let's go and check them out then. And I'm telling you Bobby – you *will* see perfection today. I'm telling you. That's a promise."

"We'll see", Bobby said giggling as the three of them got to their feet and followed Webby across the field to the Prog Stage.

Left-Hand Orcs played a forty-minute set, their music reminding Webby of the band *Focus*, without the yodelling. Up next B*lue Purple Winwood* walked on to their intro music and began playing. He considered their Hammond organ is a little to brash. "They aren't bad", Marcus mused as he nodded his head in time with the music.

The sun continued to blaze down on this Maidstone music festival site and the smell of grease and frying onions was diffusing through the stifling air. Occasionally the unique clank of a festival portable toilet door could be heard through gaps in the music.

"Told you we wouldn't see perfection today Webby!" Bobby shouts over smiling. "Greatness yes, perfection no."

The four friends and band members continued to watch *Blue Purple Winwood* for another five minutes or so and collectively decided to visit the Main Stage for a slight change of scenery and to take a break from being in a sea of camping chairs.

The Main Stage has four bearded men with a confederate flag as their backdrop. Webby assumed they were from Hull or somewhere equally as inappropriate. The bearded lead singer with the oversized hat and cut-off t-shirt sipped a can of lager, then asked the crowd to sing along to their southern rock anthem. Webby smiled, both at the cliche and at his sporadic grey chest hairs sprouting from his t-shirt. He realised he must have forgotten about that when he dyed his long hair.

Webby reflected on the words Bobby had said, not twenty minutes ago "Told you they wouldn't be perfect."

But he was wrong. John Webb knew that. Perfection was there, ever-present. You just had to look in the right places for it.

He knew it wasn't an easy task, if it was, everybody would gain it and then, if everyone had control of perfection it wouldn't be as valuable as before. But John knew where to find it. He wanted it above all else and that's simply why he always managed to find and grab it. No matter how well camouflaged or slippery it was. Or what it cost.

Webby smiled to himself again and took another sip of his drink.

Although Strychnine is a white, odourless, bitter crystalline powder, it had been placed into a small pellet earlier in the month and now sunk into Bobby's ale easy enough. He had dropped it when in the beer tent. Although he knew Bobby won't be found dead until the next day, Webby was sure they will find no motive for him to murder his friend.

And why should they? He was a good friend after all. And a hell of a bassist. No motive, no weapon.

The perfect crime. Webby had a moment of concern that they wouldn't find a bass player as good. But that was fleeting. The sun shone and today the music played. Life indeed was simply wonderful.

STICKS AND STONES

The crowd cheered below the many flashing lights above them. Many phones were held aloft recording the moment for their own viewing pleasure later or indeed sharing this moment to the world via the alchemy of the internet, as others raised their arms and sang back to the music that was being delivered to them. Although the bar area was clear enough to serve drinks, the front of the pub was what could be described as packed to the rafters with over a hundred fully grown adults squashed like sardines and as close to the stage as possible, the metal barriers providing a small gap between the stage and them. The already warm venue made even hotter. with the sea of perspiring bodies. It was like a sauna but one that played loud music, served beer, and held hundreds of joyful people thankfully with their clothes on, albeit manly with cut off denim jackets and long hair.

Ears were plugged as the bar staff continued to serve drinks and smile to the customers who were obviously enjoying the sights and sounds of the Oaks Music Bar.

As Sandra swiped another customer's card and thanked her, the large smile stayed on her face. As the manager of the Oaks she was grateful for the custom, especially in these current times with the cost-of-living crisis at full swing. As she once again basked in the satisfaction of the busy room she figured this evening would hopefully put the bank manager at bay for at least another week. Assuming that the majority would buy more drinks once the band were done indeed gave her some hope in this tough business. It helped; she knew that bands like these always almost sold out. Some bands didn't and only brought a handful of fans. If these fans were of the younger generation, they usually hardly drank alcohol which didn't do her or the bar costs any good whatsoever. But bands like these, she thought as she remained smiling, thankfully pulled in the punters - and in truth she could completely see why they did. Moving some sliced lemons to on top of a fridge, she watched as the four men on stage played what could only be described as good old fashioned classic rock and roll, the craft of musicianship and stagecraft all being executed brilliantly. Her large smile remained as she appreciated how the guitarist held his instrument like a lover, his mouth mimicking every note his fingers played, long straight blond hair sticking to his face with sweat as he continued to caress the freight board and step delicately on his pedal board. Her eyes wandered to the bass player, who seemed to be having the time of his life, his sensible short hair and polo top giving him the appearance of someone from the local sports club who had happened to walk on to the stage and act out all his childhood dreams and fantasies at once. His playing ability however showed that he knew *exactly* what he was doing. And he made it look so easy, an art Sandra knew that was way trickier than it looked. Her eyes then soaked in the man sitting hunched behind the drumkit; moving the rest of the lemons temporarily forgotten as she watched drummer, grimacing as he hit every beat, controlling the tempo of the songs with seemingly unlimited energy. The fountain of sweat rolling down his bald head and his large muscular body straining as he sat on his drum stool, he reminded Sandra of one of these blacksmiths that appeared in fantasy movies that featured dragons and castles. Once her eyes had toured the stage it stopped at the singer. Aware of the cliché but not caring she admitted defeat and accepted it was him she could not peel her eyes off. Confirming it was not solely her, she looked out at the audience (and Caroline, one of her younger bar staff) confirmed she was certainly not the only one. All eyes were firmly on the handsome sexy sweaty front man of the band. And Sandra thought to himself, he damn well knew it.

Sandra gaped as he cakewalked around the stage, strutting like a peacock. He held the microphone stand with his left hand as he held the microphone with his right, hips twisting clockwise then anti-clockwise, the movement clear in those tight ripped blue jeans of his. His long dark hair, with the dyed bleached stripe at the front, flowing back as the fan on the stage performed its function and blew it away from his forehead. Sandra was reminded of those videos she used to watch on MTV with the rock bands from Los Angeles, a diner, some cute waitresses and a fast car or two. And suds. Yes, there was somehow always foam.

As the song stopped, he swung the microphone lead away from his feet and smiled, his bright white teeth glowing through the haze of the smoke machine.

"Well, hello there. It's so great to be here in the Oaks Music bar in this incredible town of…where are we again?"

The audience laughed and many shouted back cheerfully "DEAL!".

"He's funny." Caroline turned to Sandra as she blushed slightly. Sandra agreed and watched her young employer fidget with her hair. Sandra knew who Claire would be dreaming about tonight, and knowing Claire as she did, had no doubt she would be stalking him on Facebook for the next few days.

"Deal. Kent. Of course, it is", he continues laughing after he leans down and grabs a drink from a water bottle on the stage. "My name is Steve Stones and this behind me is one of the best drummers in the world and he's in my band. What's the odds huh? Please welcome the insanely talented Tom Zhergo."

The audience cheered as the large drummer made some noise, his hands and feet seemingly moving as in fast forward, the grimace deepening as his muscular arms flail gracefully through the air.

"Thank Stonesy!" he shouted over as he finished his ten second solo. His grimace turned into a smile as he said the words, wiped his face with a towel he had nearby and re-adjusted himself slightly for the next song.

My *drummer,* he thought as he counted in for Firefly, their penultimate song, smile still covering his sweaty face. My *drummer indeed. Bloody* prick*!*

Tom watched from behind his kit as Stonesy spun around a few times, his knees reaching his elbows, one then the other as he waited for the first verse. Microphone stand firmly held in hand, audience cheering his every move Tom couldn't help thinking that he had not ever met such a stupid ignorant arrogant man in his entire life. Ever.

"This song is called Firefly, another new one. Followed by, well you know it. It's called Jack and Whack. I'll be joining you for one of the afore mentioned after the gig. It depends on who you are as to which one, ha-ha. But first - Firefly!" Stonesy said as the song built up through the monitors and the Oaks Music Bar's speakers. He then stopped lifting his legs up, pulled up the microphone stand with his left hand and pointed to the audience as he then began the first verse. The crowd laughed, danced and cheered.

Not for the first time in the last hour Tom carried on the beat and thought that Stonesy could really not carry a tune at all.

Sweat dripped down the centre of his back and carried its journey slowly into his bum crack as Tom thought back to the 'band chat' in The Hope and Anchor after the evening of auditions earlier on in the year. He recalled it was a cold evening and the studio's heating was struggling but thankfully the pub had its fire on and the flames together with the beer were the perfect tonic.

"That second guy, Stonesy. He was brill." Jake had said, tying and re-tying his long hair in and out of a ponytail as he watched the embers burn. An action, Tom knew, that was done when he felt someone would disagree with him. An action, Tom also knew, that he was right to perform.

"He *was* good. And looked the part too in fairness." Bob's quiet tones and Jake's nervousness somehow grated with Tom, who was sitting on the other side of the table, his back to the flames. The heat felt good, but his mood was frosty.

"I thought he was all hat and no cattle," he said, his arms still firmly folded.

84

Jake and Bob attempted to look like they understood but failed, so glanced back at the pub's fireplace and its glowing centrepiece.

Finally, Jake cracked. "But Tom. He nailed every song, *and* his writing does seem to go with our vibe…"

"He was shit." Tom interrupted, unfolded his arms dramatically and downed his pint. He knew it was two to one. He also knew he was on the losing side, and it was futile to argue. "Bollocks," he continued before the other two could speak again. "I know what you two are thinking. I'm going to the bar. Same again? And one of *you* can call him with the good news."

The song ended and the crowd cheered as loud as if not louder than before. As Tom looked out, he saw everyone in that moment. Living for the music. A sweaty dark room full of people, massed together, drinking, singing and enjoying themselves. All the strains and stresses of life momentarily gone away for the time they stood and watched the band. Their mortgages, their divorces, credit card bills, neighbour disputes, work woes - all forgotten for the past hour. His smile widened as he leant forward to pick up his bottle of water. As he gulped some down, his mind wandered back to that first rehearsal with Steve.

"He's late." Tom had said, sitting on his drum throne behind the studio's kit and deliberately prodding his watch. "It's his first rehearsal and he's late. Christ, these rooms don't come cheap you know."

"Give him five minutes," Bob mumbled and pretended to check volume knobs on his bass, "he may have got lost."

"It's two minutes from the tube stop. Anyway, let's start with Rancid Taste and hope he comes soon. Money doesn't grow on trees, and we have only have two hours."

Tom recalled Steve Stones did come through the door, fifteen minutes late, can of lager in hand and no apologies on the cards. In his defence he got straight to the equipment, picking up his microphone and stand and getting himself sorted without a word of complaint, immediately going through various lyrics and changes that suited his vocal range without any further fuss. But being late on your *first* rehearsal. *Come on*, Tom thought as he brought himself back to the present and counted them in for their last song. He watched Stonesy take a sip of his beer and grab the microphone stand like a cheerleader's baton. Damn it, he should have done more to say no at the first audition, been more vocal about his doubts. Yes, been more authoritative maybe? But he supposed he was here now and at least the crowd appeared to love all the new songs that Steve had brought along with him in the writing process.

Sweat continued to pour from his forehead as he felt his t-shirt cling to his chest. He pounded away at his drums, arms and legs on muscle memory as he watched the other three members in front of him, one more visible in his sight than the others. As his arms swung and his feet tapped, his mind whisked him away him back to when they played Savfest. What a festival that was. A fantastic day and a cracking set. Although how they managed to pull off that set was pure luck, he mused. He recalled twenty minutes before showtime, the band needed to be on stage for a quick line check and to talk to the sound engineer about some issue or other regarding a dodgy cab. The three of them were there, of course they were – but one (no bonus prize for guessing who) was missing. Ten minutes or so later, Jake managed to spot Steve at the bar with two beautiful women. In fairness he was selling them merchandise, but the constant schmoozing was completely unnecessary, Tom figured. Didn't he *know* they had a job to do first? Like *their fucking job.*

Was that the same day of the interview for the new upcoming rock bands magazine? Tom thought about it and realised yes; it probably was. In fact, yes it was because he remembered the cluttered backstage area and how it smelled of damp and cigarette ash. The interview with the young female reporter with the bright pink hair and the annoying voice who only focused on Steve. Steve told her about the songs and the song writing process and the production and the touring schedule. Steve told her how much fun he was having and the bands he enjoyed on the current circuit. It seemed to be only Tom that noticed she failed to direct even one question or give any sort of credit to the rest of the band. Tom remembered it well. It was apparently the Steve Stones show featuring his three stooges.

Tracking back to the here and now, Tom's mind was aware of the present. The audience were buzzing with excitement and Tom did have to admit they were doing one hell of a job tonight. They were as tight as they ever had been and even the hiccups in rehearsals had ironed themselves out. This good thought soon dissolved in his mind when Stoney's mic stand, currently spinning in the air as it was being twiddled by left hand, missed his cymbal by mere inches.

"Prick," he mumbled to himself as the chorus kicked in. The audience sang along "J-a-a-a-c-k and w-h-a-a-a-a-k. Gimme Jack and Wack. I need a stack of Jack and w-h-a-a-a-a-a-a-c-k!"

Again, the mic stand spun in the air inches away from him.

"OI! Get away from my motherfuckin' drums!"

As the words roared over the stage, he noticed from the corner of his eye Jake and Bob steal a worried glance behind them, then carry on with this final song. Steve was too busy prancing on stage, Tom noted, to even notice the anger aimed at him and him alone.

If he pulls that trick again, Tom thought as he carried on pounding at the drums, *God help me I will punch him in the face. I don't care who sees.*

Lucky for Tom, Steve and all involved, he didn't.

"Thank you Deal!" Steve shouted as the crowd all raised their arms in the air and applauded. Tom stood from his drum stool and together with the band walked off the stage and straight to the merchandise table. Job done. And by all involved – a damn good one.

Tom sat on his sofa, his little baby in his lap, aware of the sound of the cutlery drawer in the kitchen being opened signalling that tea was nearly ready. He quickly clicked on the link that he had opened on his phone which was supported precariously on the arm of the sofa.

PLAY IN CAR: LIVE IN THE OAKS ROOM, DEAL.

Well, what can I say? This is the third time I have seen Play in Car and boy, they did not disappoint. The venue was choc-a-bloc, and everybody was raring to go. Condensed Matter opened up proceedings, a three piece from Cambridge. With their rock sound taking nods from their love of prog, the songs, well written were performed well. Their six-song set was perfect. For one I cannot wait to see them on a bigger stage.

Then it was the main event Play In Car. Wow. These boys know how to bring the party. Robert Jackson, Jake O Neal and Tom Zhergo played their parts perfectly. Robert plays every note clear and concise and with Jake's low-slung bass added in the mix the sound was superb. But hats off to their fairly new lead singer Mr Steve Stone. What a frontman. A hybrid between Steven Tyler and Mick Jagger, he has all the swag, all the humour and one hell of a pair of lungs to go with that. What a find he was to the band. He has previously talked about his love of the song writing process and his hard-working attitude, and that can be seen clearly through their whole set. Their new songs sit well and these well-crafted works were perfectly sold to the more-than-happy full house. The relationship between band members is a delight to watch. Tom at his drums shouting at Steve when his microphone stand went to close was both funny and well-choreographed. Both play their parts brilliantly, Tom as the foil to Steve's over-excited main role. Well done lads. Do yourselves a favour and see this band before they hit the big time. With Steve Stones at the helm, they will simply go from strength to strength.

"Tea's ready!"

Tom picked up little Alison, his phone falling from the arm of the sofa to the rug below. He lets it stay where it has fallen. He looked into his beautiful baby daughter's eyes as he held her tightly. She looked back at her daddy. Close to tears at the spiritual connection, Tom hoped she felt the warmth, love and safety he was emitting.

"Alison." He spoke gently and quietly to her. "Please don't ever be a singer."

PREY

Another car drove past, its headlights seemingly doing nothing but
highlighting the torrential rain that was falling relentlessly from the black
skies above. The sound of tyres pushing against the ever-deepening water
welcomed him as he noticed the travelling vehicles were on a go slow
tonight. The storm obviously causing concern to those who had chosen, for
whatever reason, to drive their cars through such miserable dreadful
conditions. Although driving with reasonable care, the concentration
required to manoeuvre through the flooded road safely gave him
confidence that the driver would not have noticed him. The main road in
this weather was tricky enough, on a suburban street like this, with cars
parked in every available space the concentration had to be higher. Far too
high to spot a man leaning against a small wall, his black hooded top so
wet it was clinging to his skin like cellophane. The darkness and
continuous stream of water from both the storm and the late evening had
supplied him with adequate cover. Of that, he was sure. The dark engulfed
him and even the headlights of the car would struggle to pick up the
silhouette of a man. On a dark wet evening like today invisibility was the
armour of choice. Even if the lights *did* pick him up, and even if the driver

92

did observe the soaked pedestrian, so fucking what? He or she would simply assume that there was a poor soul out there in the storm who had perhaps locked themselves out or was having to take their pet dog for a walk. There was absolutely no reason at all to be concerned.

Sticking to his legs, his black jeans clung tight, allowing no more water to be absorbed into the already saturated denim, the wind and rain battering against his whole body. He stood, feeling like a mast on a ship, hands firmly in the hooded top pocket, fists clenched. The desire to remove them and wipe the constant battering of rain to his eyes was there, but futile. Next time, he mused, waterproofs would be a better idea. Or at least proper shoes he thought as he looked down at his canvas trainers as they stood on the pavement, a small trickle of water now not only around them but running over the top of them. He could feel his sodden socks weigh heavy on his feet squelching every time a move was made.

The man looked up again, at the house in front of him. Not directly in front but two houses to his left. From his vantage point was the perfect view, and he was sure he was hidden from sight by a parked car and a recently planted sapling. Hidden from view, that was, if she actually decided to look out of her bedroom window. And that was doubtful. the curtains were drawn and the lights off. From his position, he watched the dim light through the frosted bathroom window - a light he had calculated that was coming from the living room on the other side of the house. She was undoubtedly tucked away in her living room, on that other side, sprawled on the settee with possibly a glass of wine - white was her favourite, but he knew she also occasionally enjoyed a red. Or possibly a cup of tea, milk no sugar. Yes, he agreed with his own evaluation - she would be watching some television show in the warmth and comfort and safety of her own home.

He knew the drill. This was his fourth evening out here, although the wettest. The light would go off about 11 pm, the bathroom light would go on for three or four minutes, then seconds after that one went off, the bedroom light would be switched on. That itself would go off before 11.20pm.

Although the hood remained in place, the rain still battered at his face. Deciding to remove his hands from his pockets to wipe at the film of water that was formed, he confirmed its futility. He used the opportunity to check his watch, pressing the button so the time display could be visible. The green light showed him it was 10.45pm. Another 45 minutes to wait. It would give him time to know the structure of Olivia Breeze's evenings in and out. Sighing and leaning against the wet wall, he continued to watch the occupied house in front of him.

The hotel was accessed through a swipe card and for this was he was deeply grateful. The thought of making polite conversation with someone at the desk when entering would cause discomfort. With midnight fast approaching, they may have been slightly suspicious of a man entering, drenched like a drowned rat with nothing more substantial than a pair of jeans, canvas trainers and a hoodie. The clothes may be inappropriate for these conditions and weighed down with water, but it was imperative that he could move fast if required. Core strength was good, but ease of movement was preferable in certain cases when physicality was required. Ease of movement beats brute strength every time. He knew more than most that those who struggled when exposed to physical force could not be identified simply by sight. You could predict the strugglers, the fainters, the runners from their eyes most of the time. *Most.* You simply couldn't bet on it. Everyone reacted differently when the adrenaline kicked in, and it was one of those things that, if you relied solely on your guessing game, you would be increasingly disappointed. Sometimes the wiry ones fought, the larger ones ran. This was only too well known from experience. He walked up to the second floor, swiped into the room - room 204 and placed the card in the holder. Light bathed the room indicating the card was securely inserted. Closing the door and ensuring that the security chain was in place, he decided to wait for his desperately-needed piping hot shower in order to get the last of today's jobs done. Will-power and discomfort were required, and he had suffered through both tonight. Peeling off the saturated jeans and top, his t-shirt below clung tight to his muscular chest like it was super glued. Picking up the wet clothes and throwing them in the bath, he grabbed a large towel and towelled himself, if not dry, then at least not wet.

He threw the towel on the chair next to the bed, leant down into his rucksack which was next to the television, unzipped it and removed a laptop. Opening it and placing it on the bed he then switched it on. One day, he would get to enjoy the perks of a comfortable hotel room. Its large shower, a sauna, room service, even the luxury of having the time to watch a dumb television show from the comfort of his bed. Opening *Facebook* and clicking on Olivia Breeze, he enlarged her photo. A woman looked back, a large smile on her face, rounded glasses sitting on a very small but cute nose. The photograph showed her hair to have a metallic sheen, but he knew that she had recently changed it to a more blond colour. And had grown out her fringe. After pressing the messenger button and checking whether she was online (she wasn't), he slid off the bed and removed a leather case from his rucksack, gently placing it on the bed next to the laptop. Unzipping it and unfolding it, he opened it out. Once satisfied that the door was locked and the curtains were sufficiently drawn, he admired the contents of the leather case. A pair of binoculars were strapped firmly to the inside. Removing them with a click, he checked them over, turning them in his hands a couple times then placed them back in the case seemingly satisfied. Next to them sat a six-inch blade, its handle black with grips etched in. The blade was sharp and serrated and although had been used to stab, slice and gouge many times it looked brand new. Lifting it from the case, he raised the blade to the light and again with a slight nod of head placed it back carefully in the case. The last item to be removed and checked was the small grey handgun. Lifting the pistol to his face and checking it from all conceivable angles, he clicked the safety lock off then on again, and then again with a slight nod placed it carefully back in the case. Once satisfied, the case was zipped closed and moved off the bed to the desk.

He checked *Facebook* once again before closing the lid on the laptop, then moved it to the floor, now satisfied that a warm shower and some sleep was now deserved. A long day tomorrow and a very early start meant a crystal-clear head was required. After all, things may soon get very busy. Very busy and perhaps very messy. And when matters got messy, exhaustion was unwelcome. As the motorway signs read, Tiredness Kills. He knew they were not wrong.

It had been a long time since he had switched off his alarm call on the mobile phone, rolled over and welcomed sleep back but, by God, he was tempted to do just that when, at 4.45 am, the phone vibrated and produced the most annoying of noises. Instead of turning over, his legs swung over, his bare feet reached the carpet and, with a little effort, he stood up. Slowly walking to the bathroom, he urinated loudly, flushed the toilet and put on a fresh t shirt. That damn rain better had finished its downpour, surely there could be no more rain left in the skies, that much fell yesterday. Pulling up his jeans which were still damp, and regretting not hanging them up last night, he grimaced and buttoned them. He pulled on a pair of dry pair of socks and his damp trainers soon followed by his black hooded top, again still wet from last night. It smelt slightly musty, dammit. He would have a chance to dry everything later this morning, he hoped. He slipped the room card out of its holder and placed it in his back pocket before unhooking the security chain from the door and leaving the room, a dry, warm sanctuary he wished he could spend little longer inside.

The shifting clouds cleared a pathway, exposing the bright full moon, and he quietly thanked no one in particular that the rain had finally stopped. Confidently strolling the length of Portree Road, recognising the tree and car he had stood behind for hours last night, he opened the small metal gate of No 6. Without hesitation he swiftly pulled the handle of the front door down, pushing it down whilst pulling it towards him. The resistance showed that the door was locked. A dog barked a few doors down as he released the door handle from his grip. As he snuck a glance to the upstairs bedroom window, the barking could still be heard. It wasn't quiet. The damn mutt would wake the whole street, he thought. Muttering a low "Shit" he turned around, walking away from the door, and ensuring the gate was closed, he walked back to his hotel room, the sound of barking still audible in the background.

The last two days had remained dry, the only sign of the recent downpour was piles of wet discarded brown leaves along the gutters and against hedges. He watched from the bus window as the sun attempted to break through the clouds above and shine its weak light on the hustle and bustle below it. Someone had scratched the window, but he could see the moving scenery as the bus chugged slowly along the roads, stopping every couple of minutes to pick up its passengers. Past the scratching, he saw shops opening, folks getting on with their morning business, some lifting up metal shop shutters and others putting out signs which stated what bargains were available today. He watched as the homeless stirred from their sleeping bags, the flashing lights of the refuse team making their way across the city hiding the evidence of another day.

The blue medical mask was covering most of his lower face and the black baseball cap covered the top half with its flat visor. The mask tugged slightly at his ears as he mused that the pandemic had its uses after all. The bus made a grating noise as it stopped to allow the arrival of more people. He hoped it wouldn't get too busy, as he realised the busier it was the less chance that Olivia would be talking on her phone. She was a well-mannered lady and certainly wasn't one to talk loudly in her device on busy public transport. More introvert and then extravert. His research had been thorough, of that he was sure, and he had chosen his bus seat carefully, the last week of espionage showing her daily patterns and routines. She always sat on the left and usually towards the rear. Thankfully, today was no different. He breathed through the blue cloth as he sat on the seat right behind her, three in front of the back row of seats, the ones that were harder and with more graffiti on them.

He continued to look out the window. If he was observed he would simply be seen as an anxious or medically vulnerable man watching the world go by, lost in his own thoughts as were most people on this bus. Behind the mask he was listening intentionally to every word of her conversation. Knowledge was power after all. One-sided conversations were not the perfect information catches but every detail, crucial or otherwise, was noted. Olivia was talking to Jen, her best friend – who was also on the way to work herself. He couldn't tell if she was driving her car or, like Olivia, on public transport, but she hated her job, especially her boss whom she had slept with three years ago, a move that she regretted completely now. Alcohol and relationship problems were rife at the time - for both Jen and her boss. But he thought that mattered not. What did matter, was that Olivia had told Jen that she was going to meet Fred, not Freddie she has emphasised, but Fred at 7pm at The Rose And Crown, the one next to Wilkos in the high street. Then, she had said, after a few drinks, they would probably go for tapas. Or possibly the new steakhouse which had recently opened with great reviews. She was nervous but very excited, she had stated. "Second date nerves. I know I'm like a teenager", she had giggled quietly into the phone and covered her mouth with the back of her hand.

Once he was satisfied all the information required was received, he decided to get off the bus, awareness of blowing his cover providing stealth and bit of extra care. It was doubtful but all circumstances had to be considered. As the bus turned another corner, the red button on the pole was pressed, he pushed his cap further down his head and stood up, swinging slightly as he used the metal railing to assist walking to the bus door. Quietly thanking the driver, he stepped off the bus, watching it go its merry way. The green numbers displayed the time on the sturdy watch he owned and he realised that the whole day was ahead of him. It was a long time until 7pm but preparation was required – ensuring his knife was sharp, the gun was loaded and its chamber clean, and ensuring the car was clear and parked just where it would be later, required time and plenty of it. He begun the walk back to the hotel. The preparation may take hours of patience, he thought with a sigh. Although the sounds of screaming and the sight of fresh blood and ripped gouged flesh did not necessarily faze him, tonight, he reckoned, it may be a particular messy one. And the messier and louder, the more risk of a disturbance. And disturbances were wholly unwelcomed in this game. Olivia was to stay on the bus for four more stops, that he knew, but his priority was to ensure preparations were complete for the busy evening ahead.

He would be lying if he said The Rose And Crown was his kind of place. He sat at a wooden table in the corner of the pub on what could only be described as an old wooden school chair. His meal of a steak pie and chips was ordinary, unlike the price, he mused, but in order to get here for an hour or so before, pick a perfect spot for good sightlines and not look suspicious, buying a meal had to be done without raising eyebrows. He was grateful he only had to waste twenty minutes for the ideal car parking space. Driving around the block the first three times, he was annoyed to see that a car was parked there, but on the fourth round he was just in time to see the black Vauxhall exit from it. Perfect. He parked up and walked straight into the pub, noting the timing of the journey from car to pub. Twenty-four seconds. And here he was, a selection of unnecessary, cumbersome and oversized menus causing just enough camouflage not to be recognised, thankfully. Lady luck was present today. He had however removed his cap and mask and, as he now sported thick rimmed glasses and a denim jacket, it would be a far stretch if he was recognised as the bus passenger or the street surveyor or any of the other parts he had recently casted himself as. Holding his mobile phone in his hand, staring blankly at a news feed which said nothing but trivial bullshit that no one surely wanted or needed to know, he looked as casual as he could. Giving the impression he was waiting for someone was the perfect cover, emphasised by the occasional sigh parting from his lips the moment eyes at the bar glanced his way. In truth, he couldn't wait to get this done. There was only so many pints of lime and soda you could drink without feeling like your belly was going to swell like a balloon. And the last week had been excruciatingly boring. He was very much looking forward to some excitement tonight. Action was required and it would come soon.

He glanced up subtly as the man named Fred (not Freddie, he imagines Olivia saying) with a velvet jacket and shoulder length hair walks in the pub door. He walked straight to the bar, very self-assured. Confident, he thinks. Cocky possibly? It was too early to tell. He watched over his menu as Fred ordered a vodka and diet coke from the young bartender who looked like he was just out of school. Noticing Fred was of slim build, around five foot eleven and in his early thirties, he continued to watch as Fred glanced in a mirror then paid for his drink and sat at a table with a chair opposite, in the other far corner of the pub. Perfect sightlines, he thought. In fact, he was pleased to notice that his general height and build reduced the difficulty of a big physical struggle. Although as he knew only too well, looks may deceive, it was pleasing none the less. It was difficult to imagine losing a physical confrontation with a man who sports velvet without shame. He continued to watch as Fred walked back out the front doors, returning around three minutes later, the slight smell of some vanilla essence hanging in the air.

He smiled to himself. Vaping is so damn undignified; he thought as he sipped at his lime and soda. Just so unmanly. Confidence levels raised a notch.

He was pretending to read a message on his phone when Olivia walked in, and he stole a glance upwards. Her tanned skin, glossy brown hair and almond eyes complimented that wide large smile. He lifted his eyes from the mobile and saw Fred and her hugging. Cute, real cute. She removed her jacket and scarf as Fred walked to the bar and ordered her a drink from the young bartender - a gin and tonic - double, and for himself another vodka and diet coke - single. He noticed Fred hadn't stopped smiling since Olivia walked in. With the drinks in hand, he watched as Fred sat down opposite Olivia. "Cheers," they said and clinked glasses. Fred was facing him and Olivia away from him so even if, which was doubtful, she recognised him from the bus, the street, the supermarket or the chemist, she would not spot the connection. Of that, he was sure. This wasn't his first rodeo after all. A selection of hats was always in his travel case and thankfully this week was no different. Sometimes the simplicity of disguises was amazing.

Sipping at his lime and soda and lowering his eyes to his phone again, he yet again heard their laughter and some aspects of the conversation. Hoping that Fred would feel the urge for another vape before it got too busy, he read another news article and, just like that, his luck was in, as he heard Frank say, "Sorry Liv, just going to go and get some fresh air. I'll get another drink on the way back." With that, he checked that the car keys were in easy reach in his inside pocket. They were. He knew his pistol was in the other inside pocket - again easily accessible. This might not be too messy after all. He felt the weight of the gun and stood up then, no more than ten seconds later, he also strode out of the front door of the pub, directly behind the man who called himself Fred (not Freddie), the man that sported velvet jackets and drank single vodkas. Risking a sneak at Olivia, he noticed she was already reaching for her phone. She had thankfully not recognised the man with the mask and cap. The hats and spectacles had done their job satisfactorily.

Walking out, he stood face to face with Fred – a plume of sweet-smelling smoke rising from his mouth.

"Hi mate," he said smiling through the vanilla essence, "least it's stopped raining."

He picked up a slight West Country twang to his accent, but only a little. There was no time to ask. Or inclination. He immediately pulled out the pistol, the silver barrel pointing directly towards the velvet jacket.

"What the..." Fred's smile stopped cold.

"Don't say another fucking word. Walk!"

"You've mis…"

"Walk!" he said again through gritted teeth, and prodded the gun so the

barrel poked into Fred's chest. "Now."

He watched Fred's vape drop to the ground as he talked, quicker than he

did inside to the barman, "If you want money, man, I have…"

He recognised that the pitch had also risen alongside the speed of his

vocals.

"Move!" he simply repeated.

Fred turned around and immediately did what he was told. The man

ensured that he could feel the barrel pushing against the velvet jacket in

the centre of his back. Both men walked away from The Rose and

Crown. With one hand on the gun, he used the other to reach for the car

fob which was still in the inside pocket of his jacket. Clicking it, the

relief flooded when he heard the familiar beeping sound. However, he

restrained a smile. There also happened to be nobody around, not a

soul. Things, it seemed, had so far worked out just dandy. But

relaxation was not an option. Not yet. Not quite.

"Get in the car," he spoke.

Fred knew which car he meant. He had seen and heard the flashing

lights and the sound of the Mini unlocking. The black new Mini,

inconspicuous in its normality, parked conveniently just outside.

"Keep your mouth shut and I'll explain everything."

Pulling open the car's back door, he watched as Fred stumbled

in ungraciously. Fred rolled a little but managed to squeeze his knees

behind the driver's seat and get himself in a seated position. He didn't

take his eyes from the gun which was still pointing at him.

Fred wanted to speak, to shout, to scream even but his throat was

dry. It felt raw. He felt a little urine roll down his leg. As the warm fluid

soaked into his skin, he continued to stare at the man with the denim

jacket and the horn-rimmed glasses who was standing on the pavement

at the open car door, holding a gun inside the car, its barrel merely

inches from his face.

Fred watched as the man quickly glanced around him, then

straightened his arm. Noticing that the man's finger was pulling at the

trigger, he tried to scream, but the finger moved. The trigger was pulled

three times but he only heard the first bang. Fred's pain didn't last long.

Within five seconds he felt nothing.

The man quickly looked at Fred slouching at the back of the car, a hole through his chest and two through his face. The velvet jacket and shirt were now black with blood, and he wondered if a bigger car would have been a preferable idea. It would certainly take a while for the formal identification to take place. He assumed Fred had no teeth left. Glancing around again quickly he closed the back door of the mini and casually walked back into The Rose and Crown, pressing the fob. He was once again rewarded by the satisfying locking noise. This time he did allow a smile.

Sympathy was given slightly to whomever initially opened the car, he knew the stench of human entrails would stink to high heaven but needs must. He also sympathised with whomever must eventually clean the upholstery. Fuck, he thought, that would be a job. It's a shame, the leather seats looked good in such a modern affordable vehicle.

Walking through the doorway, he kicked the discarded vape into a gutter. The shots, he assumed were not heard as there were no movement or shouts from the street or pub. He entered the pub and looked at Olivia looking at her phone. She looked up at him and then back to her phone. Her look of disappointment was visible. He was tempted to tell her that it was not her fault, her date had not pretended to go for a smoke and done a runner. That she shouldn't be sad, feel rejected at the turn of events. But he knew he couldn't. He mustn't. He understood the dead body would be discovered tomorrow morning at the latest when the sun came out, perhaps even sooner, but that it would be ok. By then he would be nowhere nearby. He took another look at Olivia Breeze, turned around and walked out of The Rose And Crown.

He more than understood that on a busy street like this there was surveillance around the clock, and it would be searched with a fine-toothed comb once the car and perforated body was discovered. There would be many professionals way cleverer than he was, watching every movement, every still, every single section of footage, watching repeatedly as he showered Olivia's date with bullets. They would observe his height, his gait, the type of gun, what hand he used. They would shake their head and talk of "catching the bastard", "not on my watch" and ensuring everything was worked efficiently before the media got a hold of it. but quite frankly, he did not give a shit.

They would never find him. It's a shame, he thought, that Olivia *would* be taken in for questioning. Not necessary as a suspect but for information. It would be upsetting for her. Possibly her date going for a cigarette and ditching her was not as bad than her date going for a cigarette and getting shot in the head. Yes, she would cry but that is a small price to pay, he thought, as he swiftly went back to the hotel. As he felt the weight of the gun in his inside pocket, he whistled a tv theme tune as he walked, not quite remembering the name of the show but recalling it involved a talking car and bad dialogue.

The leather case was folded up neatly in the rucksack, gun back safely inside, along with the unused knife and binoculars. Along with this, a Burberry toilet bag, some underwear and a couple of t-shirts. He had shoved his black hooded top in the bin, crumpled over a teabag and two empty sachets of milk. He knew it was a bit of a waste but compared to the car it was a drop in the ocean. And frankly it would make everything else damp if he packed it with the rest of his clothing. Sliding the key card from its holster he walked back down to reception, along the corridor that smelled of both paint and weed and placed his card in the transparent check-out box. The hotel would assume he checked out the next morning which would buy him some time. Time he did not require. He thought back to Olivia sitting there alone. Wondering if she had left yet, if she had realised he was not coming back. She may even walk past the Mini. Someone would eventually open the car door. Hopefully it would not be her. Probably tomorrow, when the light showed the interior through the glass. Whoever looked in would be welcomed by a body full of holes, flesh and blood and bits of skin and face splattered all inside the car. Like a food blender that has lost its top in mid-action. He wondered again if Olivia was on the way home. If so, he hoped that she had locked her front door. After all the world was not a safe place.

His rucksack hung from his shoulder as the light engulfed him. No matter how many times this happened, he feels slightly disoriented. Discombobulated perhaps. Knowing from experience the feeling did not last long but still, the image of his recent view clung to his retina as he slowly re-opened his eyes.

He was standing in a brightly light corridor, white light emitting from both the ceiling and the walls. There were another three or four people there so he began walking past them, with the slightest of nods in recognition. His vision had finally adjusted, the spots of light were no longer flitting around. Blinking once more he walked towards the large black desk at the end of the corridor. Sitting at the desk was a middle-aged man, his pale grey skin making his bright blue eyes sparkle even more than they should. A simple white t-shirt fitted him perfectly and his hair was tied into a very neat ponytail. For a man of advanced years, his hair was surprisingly full-bodied, the man thought as he reached the desk.

Gently placing the rucksack on the table, he said, "Sorry I left a hooded top there. It was damp."

The man with the grey skin, bright eyes and ponytail looked up at him.

"We could have dried it."

"Sorry."

"It doesn't matter. What's your number?" he asked.

"47."

"Mission complete? Successful?"

"Yes." he replied, wondering if he used hair products to retain the volume.

"Well then welcome back, Sir." The man smiled showing a mouth full of white teeth. Again, the man wondered how he looked so good for his age. If only the skin didn't give it away. "How did it go?"

"All good," he replied. "She is safe now. She will now not be a victim of Frederick Reginald Stephen. In fact, no one will now be a victim of Frederick Reginald Albert Stephen again. He is disposed of."

The grey-haired man took the rucksack, placed it on the floor carefully behind him, and exchanged it with a white envelope.

"Thank you," the man said accepting it and placing it in his inside jacket pocket.

"Well done. There are enough problems in the world without rapists and murderers. You have saved a number of people today. A job well done. Now, go and enjoy your rewards. We will call you back tomorrow with your next assignment."

"Thank you. Sorry about the hooded top."

"It fine," the old man said smiling. The smile was returned. Then he turned around and walked back down the white corridor. It was a tricky job sometimes, but he knew he was good at it. And being a guardian angel paid well. He would be lying if he said he did it for the cause alone. He smiled as he tapped the envelope in his pocket, whistling cheerily the tune of that old great American television show.

THE IDES OF MARCH

The stench of burning wood, rancid meat, and human excrement, uninvited as they are, fill my nostrils as I watch my city burn. The thick putrid black smoke fills the already stifling air, the odd red ember riding its wave as I wonder if those particular flames have risen from the Senate building to ensure I am reminded of the chaos of Rome below. I hear a piercing scream over the cacophony of noise, but it soon dies, replaced by more shouts from below. Rome, the most powerful city in the entire world, is in flame around me and I was partly responsible - yet there is nothing to be done. From my vantage point I crane my neck and witness a bunch of ragged men gather and violently kick down a large wooden door. I have a clear notion who they are looking for. Thankfully, it is not me. Standing on my balcony, closer to the wall than the edge I look down at the unfolding chaos. My toga is blackened by soot and if someone did glance up at me, they would not see the dash of purple that distinguishes me from the rabble below. Although indistinguishable, I know I should still walk away, check on Aemelia and my slaves and lock myself indoors until order is maintained. But I currently am finding the pull of voyeurism greater than the pull of safety. I am fully aware of the irresponsibility of such an action and can picture Marcus Favonius rolling his eyes.

My mind once again recalls a time when the games were at hand and we stood watching the entertainment below us. I stood there as Caesar and Crassus drank wine and laughed until some spilt on the marble floor. I attempted to tell them about one of his servants who had been the unfortunate victim of one of his angry mount's hooves, but the anecdote had washed over them, and I stood there feeling as invisible as one of the homeless the city swallowed up year on year. I was and am a well-respected man of the senate, and this was not the first time that day I had been made to feel like I was nothing but air. I am sure they recognised each other's slaves more than I!

I grimace as I remind myself of my last visit to my favourite licenced house in the Great Market, my usual girl could not recall my whims.

And to think I was even in attendance that fateful day when Cassius visited Marcus. The day that we discussed a plan that would change the world. Yes, Cassius did all the talking but I was present, nevertheless. He had trusted me, not Tillius nor Pontius but me. I feel another hot ember reach my folded arms and realise that the plan did indeed change the world. We saved the world from a tyrant and all they can do is destroy. I had understood the importance of the meeting with Marcus Brutus. I know that planting a seed of murder is a dangerous act to play but at least then Rome would know my name. They would all know who I am and hold their head high as I passed. The deed had been done. And they still did not recall who I was and what I have given to this greatest of cities.

I had been involved in making decisions for the people of Rome for decades, sat with my fellow senators and still when I walked up these great steps not one person lower than me even considered me a man of power. If it wasn't for our distinguishable toga, I doubt I would even have been allowed to enter sometimes.

I think back to waiting in the theatre of Pompey. Aware of Marcus's gladiators outside and aware of what we were about to do. I wanted so much for the great Gaius Julius Caesar to look into my eyes and recognise me on his final moments on this earth. Marcus Brutus, Tillius Cimber, Suetonius, Decimus Juniua, Cassius, Labeo, Aquila, Basilus, I and fifty others would be the saviours of Rome and we would be all worshipped by the citizens for removing the thorn in our side.

Recalling the moment inside the Theatre of Pompey I feel a shudder

although the burning air is stifling. The moments before his arrival are a

blur but I can remember walking into Senate House quietly with the

others, our thoughts all present in our slow methodical movements. The

noise of the crowd from the gladiator games was ever present and I am

thankful that it was. The silence I fear may have changed everything.

Recalling every single moment as I and the rest of the Liberators stood

over the fallen figure of Gaius Julius Caesar, I wipe my hand over my

face. I know I will never forget how one man could hold so much red

liquid in a body. As his blood splattered against my robe and my face

and flowed over my sandals, I had felt the need to vomit. But I didn't.

In this esteemed company I wouldn't have dared. The sound of retching

could be heard but I am grateful for the commotion outside the walls

and the noise that it carried. The company of men I had kept there

would not have forgiven me for showing such weakness. My knife had

made at least three cuts. And every one of these was made, although I

would not admit this to any soul, not for anger over his arrogance to

rule the Empire or even how he had unvalued us all at the senate. No,

every slice I had given this tyrant was made because he did not know

my name. Even when I sliced at him, I saw his pale watery eyes stare

hopelessly at Cassius or at Brutus. As I stole a glance, I saw Cassius look away. Brutus had eyes only on our poor victim. As Caesar's mouth bubbled with blood, I think he said something in Greek. But it was not aimed at me. It was aimed at Marcus Junius Brutus. Even when I felt a tendon tearing as my blade sliced him through the material of his toga, he barely noticed me.

I continue to observe the fires burning and the looting that Rome is suffering. The Senate House is engulfed in flames and the streets are as dangerous as I have ever seen and ever want to see again. I wonder what steps that pompous man Mark Anthony will take, and I realise in fact that I don't care. Above the mayhem and the shouts, the screaming and the burning I hear chants for Caesar and ponder how one man can have such following even after he is left for dead in a puddle of his own blood. I have no idea what they have done with the body. They shout his name. The King of Rome. We saved Rome from a tyrant and still I am anonymous. These damn peasants know nothing but to kneel to those who rule over them. Throughout the discord they are baiting for blood. And they have had it, although not as much as they would like. Would the blood of the senators appease them and calm Rome? I doubt it. Cassius and above all Marcus Brutus are in more mortal danger than I suspect they ever would have known. I have been informed that Cassius has wisely fled. I was also informed reliably that Cimber's body was found impaled earlier in the day. The baying crowd had celebrated at the sight of a senator in such an undignified fashion. What has Rome become?

I continue to stand at the balcony, and it dawns on me that the being forgettable, something which I have resented for so long, is, ironically now keeping me alive. Anthony's pardon meant nothing and the Liberatores are now dead men walking. The ones who have lived so far. I fear the numbers are in double figures who have been punished by the monsters below. But not me.

As I continue to watch my city burn into ashes a smile slightly forms on my face. Perhaps anonymity has its advantages.

The flames continue to rise into the sky as I hear Aemelia call me. I step inside into the safety of my own home. I think we have changed the world and my part in it will never be told by scholars. My name will never be passed on to the future generations who will sing songs about how Rome was saved from tyranny. But the price to pay for anonymity is high. As I go and hold my wife, at least I know I will live to see another day. As the Ides of March will be told in the history books. I will not be even a sidenote in this important chapter of the world. instead, I will live, as will my family. My sons will have sons and so forth. Perhaps I am blessed after all. No one would remember the name

of Casca Longus, but my lineage may still live on if the gods decide.

And I feel they may.

CURRICULUM VITAE

Lunch Atop a Skyscraper, the 1932 black and white photo hung on the grey wall of the waiting area and Bryony Springsford assumed she wasn't the first person to look at the eleven ironworkers and wondered what their individual stories were.

The table against the wall contained a coffee pot, urn, a bowl of fruit, a milk jug covered over with clingfilm, some sliced up sandwiches and three packet of crisps. The crisps, she figured would remain untouched. Noone wanted to walk into an interview covered with crumbs.

"Any plans for the rest of the day?"

Bryony glanced at the older woman who was sitting in a chair on the opposite side of the room and smiled. With grey hair tied up in a top knot, and large glasses dominating her small face, Bryony noted the lady's casual-smart dress sense that included shoes made comfort rather than design. She smiled back whilst holding her paper cup in both hands and said "Oh, I don't know, keep on looking for more jobs maybe. Or possibly just put up my feet and get a gameshow in."

As they both shared a smile Bryony knew that this woman here wasn't the main threat. It was the young blond currently in the interview room. The one with the designer heels in which she walked confidently and the large smile showing white teeth. It was the blond that would either give Bryony a reason to celebrate or a reason to cry. Briony carefully sipped at her water thinking back at the painful moments of these awkward processes.

Her mobile had rung with an unknown number within minutes of getting home last Monday.

"Hi is that Ms Springsford."

"Yes, this is her."

"Well, firstly thank you for attending the interview today here at Young and Jacks Solicitors. I know these days are a little fraught," the polite sounding gentleman on the phone said. "But I'm afraid we cannot offer you the job this time. It just came down to a couple of points. Your answers, although solid lacked any sign of real initiative. But we do wish you all the luck in the future."

Bryony had cried solidly for an hour. Sitting on her sofa and sobbing into a cushion. The week before that she had been politely informed in person that she had not made the cut.

"Sit down. Thank you so much for all your time and effort today. Unfortunately, in this industry we must take risks daily and manage these risks. We don't believe you would be the right candidate for this position, but we do thank you for all your efforts. Would you like to grab a bottle of water on the way out?"

"No, thank you." She kept her smile up for as long as she could. As she departed through the glass revolving doors and into the high street the tears pushed through and she sobbed all the way home, her fellow bus passengers keeping their distance.

Sitting and supping at her water making polite conversation with the other candidate, Bryony wondered why they could not just e-mail or text her these rejection notices. Being told you were not good enough to work alongside them was hard, being informed in person was brutal.

It was at that moment the door opened and out walked the younger candidate, her blond hair flowing, the large smile still wide on her tanned face. Behind her a smaller woman put her head around the door and said, "Margaret. Would you like to come in please?"

The older woman stood up and Briony smiled at her, mouthed good luck, and watched as the candidates' swapped positions, one walking into the room looking nervous, the other sitting down confidence oozing. Briony attempted some eye contact. "How was it?"

"Oh, you know, horrible," she replied. "They told me to wait here as I think they will let us know before we go home."

'Great,' Bryony thought as she stood up towards the table.

"Tea or coffee?" she asked and as she reached the table. "I think you might deserve a cuppa."

"Oh," the blonde woman seemed surprised. "A black coffee please. Thank you so much... so what's your plans for the rest of the day? I suppose it depends on the outcome."

Bryony answered, her back still to the young blond candidate as she retrieved a plastic cup and lifted the coffee pot. "I don't know yet really. I think I may give myself a little break. I'm hoping to finally jump a hurdle or two."

She passed the coffee to her and sat back in her seat. The woman accepted it, thanked Bryony and Bryony smiled, waiting for her name to be called.

Staring up at the eleven ironworkers again she wondered if they had sons or daughters, and if so, did they have the artwork up on their wall. Did these eleven workmen ever get told they lacked initiative? Briony occasionally shared a small smile with the woman opposite her as she sipped her coffee, as she waited. Eventually, which to Bryony seemed like an eternity the door opened, and Margaret came out. Bryony noticed Margaret was close to tears. She then saw behind her the same woman as before appearing and say, "Okay Bryony. Would you like to come in?"

She glanced once more at the candidate drinking coffee, at Margaret was who walking towards her seat, chin slightly lowered and followed the smaller woman into the office door.

A tall man with a show of his large hands invited her to sit. The table was large, and she sat opposite him and a well-dressed woman, at a guess in her early thirties. The door closed and the smaller woman sat down, pen and paper in her hand. She sat away from the other two, giving the impression she was an impartial notetaker.

"Hello Bryony. I am Stephen Merchant and this is Alex Fhamini. We are partners in the company. So, tell me what makes you suitable for this job?"

Bryony took a breath, looked at them both over the table and begun talking. "Many things," her smile widening. "For one, I listen to feedback and take it whole heartedly on board. I show…"

As she continued, the empty ricin capsule remained in her inside pocket. Adding the powder into the coffee was easier than she had anticipated.

126

Yes, she had rehearsed at home dismantling capsules from painkillers and filling them with sugar. Then placing the sugar into a hot drink, It had taken many practices to stop her hands shaking and to perform the task so it appeared effortless. Briony quietly hoped that the candidate's family and friends didn't suffer with her death too much, but job hunting was a tough business and as she had been told many times, initiative and risk-taking *was* required.

WELCOME HOME DARREN SHINE

The gentle, politely unobtrusive voice with the RP English accent cut through the fog in his mind as he slowly began to identify the words being spoken to him. The non-regional standard accent was repeating the same sentences over and over and with each repetition, the words found an increasing hold. The sentence was finally beginning to break through the chaos in his head. Images flashed then departed as quick as they came, feelings opened themselves up and vanished almost immediately in the ether. Facial features were nearly made out but as soon as they formed a definite image, they disintegrated into nothing, soon to be replaced by more such images. Rinse and repeat. Rinse and repeat. The fleeting images and the mist in his head slowly being punctured by the voice with the repeating sentences. He eventually clutched the words, ordered them somehow, and began to find meaning in the pattern of sound.

"Darren. Wake up. It's time to wake up Darren. Easy does it. Darren Shine. Easy does it. Wake up."

Faces now clearer in his mind's eye. Fleeing past as names of places and people took hold. A vision of his mum reaching down to him and picking him up in her arms to be replaced by him looking out to thousands of people all singing at him. The images all came and went fleetingly and with more resolution. He recalled that he inhabited a body, physically strong, brown hair, tattooed white skin, perfect teeth, and sharp blue eyes.

"Darren. Wake up. It's time to wake up Darren. Easy does it Darren Shine. Easy does it. Wake up. "

Eyelids twitching as he opened his mouth, his lips feeling dry but not uncomfortable, aware of his breathing gradually changing as the voice continued to repeat the sentences in the soothing tones of a gentle lover. Darren Shine opened his eyes and as the mental mist dissipated, he remembered who he was and where he was.

Laying as naked as a jaybird, the warm viscous fluid gathered around him, smothering the base of his back and half his legs.

 He glanced down at his arms and knees, above the fluid - somehow knowing that he would observe wires connecting from these limbs to the inside of the tank he was laying in. The glare calmed down and slowly his eyes began to focus on the wires in question. Also, aware that the depth of the liquid was decreasing, draining away from his bare bottom, he let out a deep sigh. Following this sensation, he closed his eyes being cautious of sensory overload and then opened them seconds later as his breathing calmed. Still facing upwards, tubes and wires of various thickness protruding from his arms, legs and one from his neck, he took another deep breath and attempted to clear the last remnants of the fog in his mind noticing the soothing voice had stopped. He wondered when it had.

The memory of thousands and thousands of people in front of him watching his every move formed. He remembered raising his arm in the air and told them that he loved them all. The crowd cheered and shouted the same back to him. Ecstatically they applauded. They wanted the encore he then offered them. He recalled he had accommodated their wishes and performed it. Of course, he had. It was the ballad that gave him the big-time. The pop music smash hit that they all had paid to see and hear. The ballad that made him a household name. The song that every phone in the audience would be held up on, flashes on, lights swaying from side to side like a wonderful meteor storm. The ballad that got him that gig on the reality TV show, which in turn opened the door for the Hollywood movie role which then led to the marriage to the leading lady. Being an internet sensation and on every celebrity gossip journalist's lips soon led to the high-profile divorce which in turn led to the re-release of the ballad in question leading to larger audiences and a wider fan base. Of course, he would finish with the ballad. It began and ended and begun there again.

The liquid had all drained away and although viscous, Darren was surprised he did not feel stickiness on his bare flesh. Continuing to lay there as a slight vibration rippled through the tank, he slowly blinked, his eyes straining a little from the glare of the brightly lit ceiling.

He recalled the conversation. "Are you sure Darren? This is big."

Stanley Kupper was sitting next to two other men, one wearing a white laboratory coat, which Darren felt was a tad dramatic, and the other was a man of African heritage, his well-groomed beard suited for his chiselled face. His choice of outfit more appropriate, a smart dark suit with no tie.

 Kupper, his reliable, knowledgeable, and very savvy agent wore his usual attire. A white shirt, red braces, and a red bowtie. He repeated himself. "Are you sure Darren? This is big."

"So is the tumour. I want to live forever. Yes, I am."

Stan had picked up the pen and signed the paper.

"Look, I know you departed on bad terms Daz, hell the whole world knows you did. But think about Orange and Lemur. These are nice kids. With the cryogenic costs, they won't get a penny," Stan flicked at his hair like he always did when he was telling Darren some hard facts he possibly didn't want to hear.

Darren just shrugged.

The decision was a simple one. Die of cancer or be cryogenically frozen.

They told him that they would put him under within the next two weeks. He accepted the terms happily with no further questions.

Now his eyes adapted to the bright glow of the ceiling, and he began ever to slightly to gently roll his naked shoulders. Aware of the goosebumps forming, Darren not only felt a little cold but very vulnerable in this metal container. He assumed the roof of the cryogenic tank had slid open when he was still 'under' as he couldn't see it from where he was laying. Although now getting restless he was more than aware of the connection to the wires and the dangers perhaps in moving swiftly. The voice began again.

"Mr Shine. Welcome. I will show you a short presentation which will last approximately twenty minutes. Then you may ask me questions. I will then begin the process of unwiring you. May I ask, and this is imperative, that you do not fidget with the wires at this stage. Please remain in your horizontal position. Sudden movement may cause malfunction and, after ninety years of hibernation, now would not be a good time for malfunctions to arise. I will inform you when you can move and sit up. This is imperative for your safety. Do not touch the wires. Please do not worry, we will look after you here on your final stage of your journey with Cryogenic Solutions Ltd. We will aim to be back into the Earth's atmosphere within four hours. I assure you by then you will feel refreshed and up to date with the procedure. Tomorrow you will receive one final health check and you will be back home. Safe, sound and altogether comfortable."

Darren Shine licked his lips as a large screen lowered down from the ceiling The volume and brightness temporarily overwhelmed him.

Darren recalled when he was younger watching these travel information broadcasts to persuade tourists to travel to destinations they had fallen out of love with. Welcome to the Tourist Board of Future Earth he thought as he had the desperate urge to scratch his bare buttocks.

A picture of Earth filled the screen, the most famous picture of Earth ever photographed – Earthrise by Bill Andres during the historical Apollo 8 mission. The Earth then formed into a clearer image of the planet, an HD image with resolution so clear Darren felt he could reach up and touch it. Slowly narrowing its lens, it began focusing in on Europe. It hung there for a while as the commentary begun over the visuals.

Welcome to Planet Earth. It's been a while. Well maybe not for you, but for us. We've missed you. The date of your arrival will be Wednesday 24th

June. Twenty-One Eighteen. And Earth is still the beautiful place you left behind all those years ago.

The camera panned over the UK and zoomed into somewhere Darren assumed was around the Bristol area.

Since you last left many things have changed. Yet many things have stayed the same. You will receive more information later today but this presentation will show you the highlights. Please continue in your comfortable position and enjoy the screening. Please ask your assistant with any pressing questions once this presentation stops, but until then look up, enjoy and let the excitement commence. Your new life starts here.

Due to what is now referred to as the overconfident misstep and ever since then - London is still mainly uninhabited. So, our capital city is the wonderful Bath. Bath is a beautiful area, with a population of approximately 3 million. When you land, you can visit the great statue of Gerwyn which is situated near our landing site next to the Crewe Crossroads. The Crewe Crossroads is a hugely important structure, now sixty-five years old, that held historic importance in the Covid fight. When Covid-19 first hit, it caused inconvenience and death, and you will soon learn about the devastating fourth wave. However, there is light from this dark tunnel. The Crewe Crossroads was where the Prime Minister and the

134

government shielded whilst making plans to halt the spreading of the strain. It was here that the order of mask-wearing and social distancing became mandatory and here four long years later that the decision to go to war with certain opposing countries was made by our Leader Prime Minister Gerwyn in retaliation for weaponizing the virus. You can of course visit his statue and from a safe distance pay respect to him. Next our virtual tour takes us to the art and culture centre of the UK. Braithwaite is a whole city dedicated to the arts and sports. It holds the main auditorium for sport and music and, as a loyal customer of Cryogenics Solutions Inc. you will have two tickets for any performance of your choice. Yes, completely on us. Each performance is safe with each member of the audience in their own comfortable and heated isolation booth. With a clear view of the stage and adjustable volume control in each booth. each performance is a delight auditorily and visually. Great music, comfortable and virus safe. The perfect day or evening out.

Darren twitched his fingers then slowly spread them out. He felt the plastic wires connecting him fragilely to the tank. As he continued to listen to the presentation he consciously began to pull at the wires.

WAITING FOR THE PUNCHLINE

Trevor shuffled his feet again, trying and failing not to focus on that feeling of his bladder expanding. God, he needed to relieve himself but *surely* his bladder must be empty by now. Three times in the last fifteen minutes the toilet had been visited and at least six times since his arrival here, and every single time no more than a dribble escaped. Inhaling a deep breath, Trevor attempted the technique that one of those self-development books had explained. The book had been purchased three or four years before, so that he could "make You the best version of You, You could possibly be", that was what the blurb claimed anyway. *Breathe*, Trevor thought, *In through your nose and out of your mouth. Or was it in through your mouth and out of your nose? Damn it, which was first?* Bloody hell, a re-read should have been done last night. Nose first, mouth first - who knew? Trying both ways one after the other did not help. The overwhelming feeling was not of calm but of the urge to choke. And yet still the urge to urinate. Looking down at his red converse trainers Trevor Mackay-Stephens leant down and touched them both with the index finger of his right hand. Feeling his leg muscles stretch and counting to five, he closed his eyes and opened them again hoping the movement would somehow bring some calm and control of bladder movements. It didn't.

Listening to the compere talk to someone in the audience, Trevor stretched his arm behind his neck. The sound through the speakers seemed slightly distorted from this angle but he could hear something about a Meat Loaf song. Trevor stretched out both arms and wished the compere would introduce him before he urinated.

"So, you would do anything for love but not do that." The slight laughter trickled to the side of the stage where Trevor heard it, staring back down to his converse and desperately trying not to bring out the folded piece of paper from his back pocket which held all the information he had needed for the next five minutes. Currently he didn't know which urge was the strongest. Removing the paper or going to the bathroom for the seventh time. Trevor resisted both and mentally urged tonight's host to quicken the pace.

Only two hours. A mere one hundred and twenty minutes, yet it seemed to Trevor, standing side stage, heart racing, nerves jangling, like a lifetime ago that he had left the house. He recalled in his mind's eye Mandy rolling her bright blue eyes as Trev pulled on his denim jacket and left the house. "See ya kids", he had shouted up the stairs.

"Where are you going, Dad?"

"Your dad's having a mid-life crisis," Mandy shouted from the living room. "He's going out to tell his knock-knock jokes to some poor people who have nothing better to do with their lives."

Trevor had made a casual snorting noise, a half laugh, a half sigh and said, "Love you dear," before leaving the house. The comment by Mandy, although not as barbed or malicious as it may have sounded, still slightly hurt. A sucker punch to the ribs, Trevor would have called it.

Three weeks ago, when watching a gameshow host talk patronisingly to three contestants, Trevor casually mentioned the idea to Mandy of performing stand-up, stating it was something he had always wanted to try. Faced with the words, "silly", "embarrassing" and "mid-life crisis" during the elimination round of the gameshow didn't dissuade him, but he had hoped for a more positive outcome. Possibly throughout the last few days he felt these descriptions were all accurate, but other times they seemed unjust. He decided that stand-up was going to be attempted, mid-life crisis or no mid-life crisis. It did not change the fact that it was something Trevor had really wanted to do for several years now. And as the books kept on telling him, life was short, experiences are priceless and being on your deathbed with regrets is a no-no.

"Why on earth would you want to stand up and have people think you are a fool?" Mandy had said when he had told her he'd booked himself a spot on the beginners' open mic night.

Trevor simply shrugged off the response from his wife and continued sipping the tea he was holding. As Emmerdale boomed through the living room, he realised that she would never understand why he needed to at least try it and, even if he could find the exact words to explain, he didn't think he would even bother.

Sneaking a glance at the stage and seeing the microphone stand, caused his mind to swiftly return to the here and now, the sensation of a full bladder making itself known again. Reason quickly replied that simply could not be the case and that the bladder was exercising its flight or fight response. Trevor glanced back at the unmanned microphone stand. Will he use it? Is it a good prop or simply a security blanket? Was he overthinking it? Maybe he should instead look at his notes? The compere was still talking to a woman about, well he didn't know what exactly, he just wished he would hurry up and call out his name.

He recalled the last time he last made his wife laugh. Was it this year? Last year perhaps? He couldn't recall. Trevor did remember however how Mandy lifted up her chin and tilted back her head back when she laughed

139

at a repeat of Only Fools And Horses on the Dave channel a few months ago. But when did he have that effect? Was it when her sister had come over and they bought a take-away as they had run out of pesto? Come to think of it, was it him or her sister that had got Mandy into hysterics that time? Mandy had literally cried with laughter and caught a small dose of the hiccups straight afterwards, which made her laugh even more. He was sure it was *him*. Well not a hundred percent sure but *pretty* sure. As Trev's mind jumped from thought to thought, his vision locked again on his converse as he questioned the last time he had made a choice for the family? Trevor was momentarily surprised with that leap of thought from laughter to decision-making, but went with it nonetheless. It seemed to take the focus off his bladder at least. He knew the opening gag should be dominating his mind, the one that he proudly wrote on the train last week on the way back from work. The joke about him resembling the TV personality who tells off conning companies and warns the public about cowboy traders, however his mind was being even more skittish than usual. Another laugh came from the audience as he briefly recalled the last four family holidays they had enjoyed - Valencia, Cyprus and Benidorm twice. Were any of them his suggestions? They *had* discussed them that was for sure, recalling the times on the laptop looking at blue skies and discussing the benefits of all-inclusive deals with the children. But now thinking on it he wouldn't have recommended any of these destinations. Would he? No, it was a *joint* decision. It must have been. They were a family, a unit, and a partnership. This was no different than when his ancestors got chased by wild beasts. Hormones don't change. The environment does. Yes, it was just his nerves giving him hell and wanting him to get out of this perceived dangerous situation. It must have been a joint decision - like the kids' names. And the colour they finally decided to paint the front door. *Joint decisions.*

Trevor listened to the compere chat (albeit slightly one-sidedly) with the audience over one of their hair styles, the slight clunking from the speaker indicated that the compere had put the microphone back in its stand. Trevor took a deep breath through his mouth then his nose, his bladder all but forgotten.

He touched his fingers to the tips of his converse again, straightened up and relaxed the shoulders. For a reason unbeknownst to him, he recalled trying to persuade Mandy that Oggy and Bruce were going to the Download Festival in summer and, for old times' sake, he would love to join them. Three school mates catching up, putting the world to rights, and of course watching their favourite band in the world, AC/DC. It was a non-starter. "We haven't got the money, Trev. You know that. We can go out somewhere together if you like. Maybe Pizza Express or even a day trip to Buxton or Bakewell. Anyway, you are a bit old for all that silliness." At the time he realised she was of course right; it was expensive, and camping for three days at his age wouldn't have done his back any good. Yes, it was a silly idea indeed.

But Bruce and Oggy did go without him and loved it. They missed him, they said, but it was incredible and the stories they told sounded brilliant. Many a pint had been drunk and many a memory had been made.

Attempting to nudge his mind back to the present and failing, he realised that it was green. He hated green. It was the grey front door he wanted. The grey with a slight metallic shading. Mandy wanted green. There was a compromise, he was sure. Grey or green? They compromised, yes, he remembered now. "Well, we obviously have to agree to disagree", she has said, "so it looks like a compromise is in order."

Trevor thought of the uncompromised green door at the front of their home. Come to think about it he wanted Luke for a boy, Jayney if a girl. Not Jayne but Jayney.

"Jayney?"

"Yes Jayney."

"What about Jen, or Gemma?"

"I really like Jayney, Mandy. I think we should consider it."

Trevor loved his children more than he could ever explain. As he tore his eyes away from his feet and was poised to walk on to that stage, Trevor knew he loved them more than anything or anyone. He loved Samantha Elizabeth Mackay-Stephens and Alfie Mackay-Stephens to hell and back. He hadn't thought of the names Luke and Jayney for years. Why did that thought enter his mind now? Would the names make them different people? Would they have acted another way, behaved worse or better, loved him differently? Would Luke have not been obsessed with the movie Planes or would Jayney not love anything from J.K Rowling? He supposed their names didn't matter. Or the colour of the door. Or the fact that he missed Angus Young at the Download festival.

None of that mattered. Not one bit. He was here now. Right here, right now. Maybe there were only five people in the audience in this run-down bar in Brixton. Maybe there was twenty. Possibly there was a television scout from a cable channel who would discover him and make him a worldwide household name. Maybe five or twenty people would laugh. It didn't matter. Even if he only made one of them laugh. Or even smile. In fact, even if none of them laughed, that didn't matter either.

"Ladies and gentlemen, it's his first time so be kind. Please welcome the one and only Trevor Mackay-Stephens!"

Trevor walked on stage to the sound of applause, took the microphone from its stand and began to talk about the television personality that looks like him. Tonight, was for him. This was his time. This was his decision.

ATTITUDE OF GRATITUDE

Remember to Apply the Attitude of Gratitude and Life will soon go your way.

And send.

Richard Saka smiled as he looked at his daily twitter post, ensured it was shared to all his followers, -always hoping for a few new ones, and logged off his laptop before the likes and comments began to flood in and distract him. Extending his smile, the laptop lid closed as he stood up from behind his desk, stretched and looked out of the large east-facing window. Posting on social media and not feeling the need to scroll was a good show of self-discipline to kickstart the day. The feeling that today was going to be a good one was strong, and his instincts were rarely wrong. Teaching the mantra enough that when you felt good, you looked good and when you looked good, the world around you worked for you, he most definitely believed it. Of course, he did, he mused - it worked. How many times had he said at a seminar or wrote in one of his books that you were not just entrapped in your flesh but the world around you? But you, yourself can alter your walls. Richard, or Rich as the world now named him, always practised what he preached. Watching the sky with his bright blue eyes, he witnessed the sun's rays attempt to break through the white clouds before he diverted his gaze downwards to the land below. *His* land below. All five acres of looked-after property would have that sun beaming down on it shortly, he hoped. It was indeed a glorious sight on a summer's day. He couldn't quite catch the large figure of Dave from where he was standing, but he knew his gardener would be hard at work mowing the lawn or weeding the edges to make it look as beautiful as possible. Like himself, Rich contemplated, Dave was always early. "'I would rather be an hour early than a minute late," Dave regularly said to him when he arrived well in advance. Rich then decided that would be the morning social-media motivational post for tomorrow.

"Thanks Dave," he said quietly more to himself than the gardener.

Rich's study, or 'Ideas Hub' as he named it in his bestselling books, was a neat space indeed. The white square desk in the centre of the light spacious room simply had a slim laptop placed on it. Left of the window was one tall bookshelf, containing all his six books in many different editions, languages, and formats. A copy of *Long Walk To Freedom* by Nelson Mandella, *How To Make Friends and Influence People* by Dale Carnegie and *The Book of Joy*, *The Art Of Happiness*, *Freedom In Exile*, *Destructive Emotions* and *An Open Heart* by The Dalai Lama also all sat upright on the shelves next to his works. The Richard Saka collection included The *Life of Gratitude, Positive and Positive equals Positive, The Internal Hard Drive* and *Find the Love in your Coffee*. Their overriding connection was that they all showed the same photograph of the author on the back cover, above the blurb and the well-chosen rave reviews. The black and white photograph showed Rich smiling at the camera, his clean-shaven head and face, and his large blue eyes staring right back at the reader with an impression full of interest and playful joy. The photograph was around ten years old, but Rich was still more than happy with the image it portrayed. Excited, keen, motivated yet calm and dignified. In truth, he hadn't changed much in that time. The healthy diet, constant exercise regime and daily stretching had so far done exactly what it had set out to do. Looking at the sky one more time and observing the sun's rays gradually finding their way down to the surface, Rich smiled and left his Ideas Hub, heading downstairs to hopefully grab a lovely freshly brewed coffee with Kate before his meeting.

"You got everything you need, darling?"

"Yeah, it shouldn't be long. An hour tops. We'll just sign off on the deal and all good. A four-book deal on 400 up front and *they* are paying for the meal." He smiled and accepted the mug of steaming coffee that she had passed him. "Thank you. Smells lovely."

Kate's smile must be the most beautiful Rich had ever witnessed, he thought for the hundredth time over the cloud of steam that was now diffusing through the air. The aroma was wonderful. Kate and he had met five years ago at his second book launch and since then he was adamant he had never seen such a beautiful smile, a fact that he continually recalled to the world in his speeches on gratitude and attitude. Rich recalled that question and answer session like it was yesterday. He was reading out the second chapter of *The Internal Hard Drive* to the selected audience of sixty people and had glanced at one of the employees of the bookstore who was presently unpacking a box. Immediately knowing she was the one. The reading and question and answer session was a success, the hour session flew and, as he was packing up his belongings and saying some goodbyes to the staff, he introduced himself to her and asked if she was free for a meal or a drink perhaps. Kate said yes, she was indeed free and the rest, as they say, is history. Two years later Rich and Kate stood in bright white clothing in the Bahamas exchanging vows. It was inevitable and, to Rich, it was perfection.

"But," Kate continued, ensuring her dark hair was still in a tight ponytail, "Didn't that Merchant guy insist on some negotiations? You don't think he's going to be a problem?"

Rich glanced at his wife, the sweat dried on her face but still wet in her hair. Her gym clothes clung tight to her and always when she had finished exercises Rich understood the term 'glowing'. He glanced at the swoosh emblazoned on her chest and wondered if the logo looked this good on anyone else.

"Don't worry about that, dear." Taking another sip of coffee he looked at her over the steam, savouring the beautiful bitter blend and its powerful soothing aroma. "I don't think he'll come. I think it will just be Matt and I."

"Fingers crossed he doesn't. He always makes these meetings difficult, "she said and leaned over through the steam to give him a kiss on the cheek. "You know best."

*

"Americana please. Oh, and a flat white for you Matt?"

"Yes please. Thanks Rich." Matt replied and smiled back at the waitress as they continued their conversation. The two men sat at the table in the Ivy restaurant, the colourful deco and upbeat music reflecting both their moods and their appearance. Although both mid-forties and the same approximate height, Matt's hair was black, thick and curly, a contrast to Rich's clean shaven smooth head.

"Well, that's it then. Four more books in the next three years and let's hope they will be as popular as the others. I'm sure they will be."

"Thank you, Matt", Rich replied shaking his hand. "I know Mr Merchant would have made the deal a little tougher, but I sure hope he's okay."

Matt smiled back at Rich, his hair bouncing slightly independently from his face. "Oh, he will be. Strangely he has been in great shape for months now but somehow managed to catch a bug or something. He got bad stomach cramps this morning he said in his texts. Came out of nowhere. He did send his sincere apologies. He hates missing meetings. Remember the last time we were meant to meet he had the same problem? Probably all that fine dining."

The men shared a laugh and looked forward to their upcoming caffeine hit.

Rich noted that the sun's rays did not only manage to break free from the shelter of cloud but stayed out for the remainder of the afternoon basking the ground with glorious light. The thought made him smile as he sat in his hotel room, three hours after his beautiful black strong coffee with Matt. His handwritten notes for tonight's talk were spread out on the king-size bed as he mouthed the speech he had prepared. The talk was named *Luck is in your Life and* the hour-long seminar was based around his belief that with the right attitude, you can make the right decisions, hence feel that luck is driving you forward which produces more good feelings. With these feelings the world is simply a better space to inhabit. The Feeback Loop of Brilliance, he tended to call it.

Rich loved preparing in this modern stylish hotel room. Although the college in which he was presenting was only ten miles from his home, his agent insisted on booking the room before the talk. Gemima has been Rich's agent for the last four years and was permanently on call. Reflecting on tonight's talk, he was grateful that he had such a kind, giving and wonderful woman for his agent. No stone was ever unturned, and her work rate was simply second-to-none. Calendars always up to date, communication always precise and accurate, problems in scheduling minimised. She was forever punctual. She and Dave would make an unstoppable team if they knew each other, and Rich laughed quietly at the thought. Three years ago, an unfortunate accident involving Gemima, her husband and a kitchen knife potentially could have got her in major trouble, but Rich and some of his team had managed to calm the waters and the situation, like most moments in time, had settled. Thankfully for Gemima time had smothered the incident from most memories. Since then,

Gemima would bend over backwards to accommodate Rich, including bagging the spacious hotel room before the gig. Gemima's husband unfortunately had made life hard for several months for her after the incident. As Gemima, Rich and the publishers began to worry about standards and reputations, her husband had met his untimely death in a freak scuba diving accident. Again, Rich was eternally grateful for the cards that he had been dealt. The publishers relaxed, the gossip died down, Gemima focused on work and everyone was productive. Gemima was indeed a godsend.

The sky was dark as the moon stuck under cover of some clouds just before 11pm. "Hi, honey I'm home."

Rich stepped through the door and was welcomed by Kate, sitting on the sofa watching a late-night movie, now out of her sports gear and sporting a red dressing gown. She picked up the remote control, lowered the volume and asked, "How was it?"

Rich smiled. He reflected at the full room, the audience hanging on his every word. He thought back on looking out to the crowd, watching as Gemima with her bright red hair and thick glasses smiled, preparing to get the books for signing out of the box and swiftly sold. He grinned as he watched Matt drink coffee from his oversized travel-mug, standing next to Gemima, happy with the sales that were soon to be made.

"It was great Kate, let me just wash my face and I'll be down to join you."

"Great." Kate smiled as Rich walked upstairs.

Instead of taking a left to the bathroom, Rich took a right to his Ideas Hub. He opened the door, walked in, and closed it thoroughly behind him.

He removed the Dalai Lama collection from his bookshelf, stacked them neatly on his desk and removed a box that sat previously unseen behind them. The box was black, no larger than an average sized tool kit. Placing the box on his desk, he glanced to the closed door again, reached into his trouser pocket, retrieved a small silver delicate key and then gently unlocked the box. Lifting the lid, he looked down into it. Facing him were eight small hand-crafted figurines. The one with the red hair had a plastic knife next to her arm. He delicately moved the knife ever so slightly from her hand. Rich carefully removed a figurine which was slightly larger than the rest and gently removed the pin from its stomach. He then placed it carefully back in the black box, the pin next to it. Closing the box, he recalled bringing one in the bath with him all these years ago, smiling as it was submerged under the water. Another, he recalled throwing out of the bathroom window when Kate wasn't home. He remembered exactly the time when he placed two figurines laying down next to each other, a bald one and a slighter smaller one with black hair. He ensured every time he opened the box that they did not move. He did not want to be lonely. The thought filled him with uncontrollable fear.

He heard Kate saying something.

"Coming dear," he shouted as he carefully lay the box back on the shelf with the spiritual leader of Tibet's book back in front of it. "Just coming down now, dear."

He was indeed grateful for all that he had been given. He sure did apply the attitude of gratitude to his own circumstance and, well damn it, life was indeed good.

AUTHOR'S NOTE

The only reasons I have written these short stories is simple. Because I, like everyone have yarns to spin. And like I said previously, I wanted to see if there were still ideas growing in this brain. These stories, if you have read them vary from subject to subject, genre to genre. One thing I have learnt in these forty-nine years on this planet is that I need to express my creative side. Be it stand-up comedy, writing novels or short stories, drawing or even compering if I am not creating, I feel a bit crap (that's the technical term I'm sure).

The tales themselves came from different places. Prey, an initial idea from Mark Parsley and influenced from Ashen Reach's great song Prey ends up being the longest in the collection. Like many it has a sting in the tail, a pattern to be found in many members of this dysfunctional family of stories. Another sting is found in New Year's Day although this nipper is subtler and to some not realised. It's one that I hope would show itself on a second reading perhaps. The shortest piece and the only piece of flash fiction is The Call. This is one of my favourite family members, although this changes daily and the first to be written in this collection. Who knows where the story will eventually lead but like every good yarn there is a million opportunities and a million destinations.

Many of these tales are optimistic and some pessimistic. I suppose it depended on what my wee brain was doing that day. Some days the sun shone and Platform 5, came to mind. Others the clouds formed, and darker ones emitted from my brain such as Attitude of Gratitude and Welcome Home. Some have surprised me. Paper Crown was completed five days before the death of Queen Elizabeth was announced. It is neither pro nor an anti-royalty story. In fact, it isn't about the late Queen at all. It's about our lives, what remains consistent and what is fluid. Fragility is a theme here. It is a theme in many others. In fact, it is probably a theme in all this collection. As individuals and a society, we are strong and resilient but also fragile. Always fragile. This fragility is clear in Beached Hen and The Call but rears its head everywhere and anywhere.

I hope, above all some of these stories have resonated with you. If, one day you are at a bus stop or a gig and you think back to any of the starring cast, wondering where they are now and what they are up to, my job here is done.

So, thank you again for the immense support you have given me by picking this book up and reading it. None of the earnings from this book are going to my pocket but to charitable causes. It's only a small act but as Bon Jovi once said, "it's the small acts of goodness that make the world a rockin' place." *

So, thank you, take care of yourself and others and enjoy the rest of your day. It's going to be a good one.

Pete K Mally

*I made that quote up. Sorry Jon

Also available from Pete K Mally via Amazon.

RESURRECTION MILL

Prologue.

18th July 1823.

The Howff Cemetery, Dundee, Scotland.

Derek McCaw kept his hands in his pockets and his collar up over his neck as he thought about those privileged few enjoying their evening, tucked up in bed in the prosperous Perth Road, overlooking Magdalen Green. He was headed the other way, north of the High Street, towards the Howff cemetery. Once, it had served as a combination of a meeting place and a burial ground. Seen as a safe haven for all, the town's Incorporated Trades meetings had been held there. People did their business and paid the respects to the deceased. Now it was simply a graveyard, its high walls designed to keep the bodies in and the criminals out. Derek walked through the slightly open gate and gave a subtle nod as he passed two burly

Charlies standing rigid in the cold night. The rain was relentless, and

the darkening evening sky reflected his melancholy mood. He pulled

his collar up further, sheltering his stubbly face from the large

droplets falling from the Scottish skies.

"Evening, gents. You would never guess it was July, would you?"

"Right enough. Mr McCaw," said the larger of the two Watchmen.

Even the weather's given up on us."

"Aye. It has indeed. Well, I hope all is quiet tonight."

As he spoke, Derek made his way past the ornate gateway towards

Barrack Street. He pushed his hands deeper into his pockets,

protecting his balled-up fists against the cold night air and his

defeated mood.

"Don't you worry, though, Mr McCaw," shouted the smaller of the

Watchmen as he turned the corner. "we'll look after them all right.

We'll keep our precious one safe, won't we, Freddie? We'll make

sure those bastards don't disrupt the dead. God bless their souls."

Aye," Freddie replied loudly for Derek's sake.

Derek heard the watchmen's dialogue and normally he would have appreciated the gesture. However, deep in his soul, he knew it was futile. Absolutely and utterly futile. He thought of Margaret, his wife. If she knew what she was about to do, he was certain it would be the end of her. *If poverty or disease didn't get them, heartbreak would*, he mused. He'd watched their son Jimmy, as he died in Margaret's arms, observing the watery diarrhoea, the vomiting and the pain on that small innocent face as the boys' muscles cramped up in his legs and lower back. Watching the life pour out of his body as he was torn inside out by such a vial putrid entity was bad enough for Derek and his wife, but the thought that those bastards would then steal his body for some posh lecture hall in Edinburgh was enough to drive Margaret mad. Derek realised that he needed to take charge. He needed to do *something*. He couldn't save his boy's soul, but damn IT, he could save *his* soul. The idea had come to him as his son lay on the cold floor, his bluish skin tight and stretched from the invading disease, his mouth still open, a little vomit on his bottom lip. He knew if he didn't act, he would regret it forever. Looking at the image that would forever be etched on his mind's eye, he made a pact that no one would use little Jimmy McCaw, his six-year-old babe as an exhibition to those toffs whose parents had paid for their spoilt upper-class brats to dissect the bodies of the young and innocent to further their so-called education. Anatomy? Butchery more like.

At the boy's funeral earlier, a crowd huddled behind him and Margaret. Derek remembered thinking how she had never looked so old, so frail. The small, cheap wooden coffin was placed gently into the ground. Derek knew that the body of his son would already be decaying inside it. He was one of the many thousands of victims of the evil scourge of modern-day sickness. As Margaret had swiped another tear from her face one more immediately replaced it. Derek once again, formed fists in his pockets, but this time he had cut into his palms with his fingernails. He'd be damned if he would let his wife see him weep. He needed to be strong. As the pallbearers placed the earth onto the miniature coffin, Derek knew what he had to do before the rain packed down the soil.

Once home, Margaret had cried herself to sleep. Derek had slipped

on his long jacket, gently closed the door behind him and walked

back to the cemetery, knowing that Alistair and Fred would already

be on guard. They were the local watchmen, or Charlies as the press

had recently named them. There were over 100 names on the

Watchmen list. Men of all ages and sizes had volunteered for the job,

but it always seemed to be the same two on sentry duty night after

night. Derek understood why this was. His own name was probably

on that list somewhere, written in a moment of defiance to the body

snatchers. When he signed it, he supposed had every intention of

doing a shift or two. But that was before cholera had gotten hold of

his only son. Everyone knew the pressure these watchmen were

under due to the uprising in bunking, but that didn't stop the wrath of

the public and the anger towards them when the grave robbers

succeeded in their plunder. Tower or no tower, lookout or no lookout

if the body snatchers got their loot, the watchmen would be target

practise for the baying mob. Derek realised it was a very unfair state

of affairs.

He had consulted with Alistair and Freddie shortly after the funeral in a quiet spot under an oak tree, while an exhausted minister consoled his wife. He told him of his idea, reluctantly at first, but with more confidence when they didn't interrupt to protest or show contempt, as he had feared they might. As each man held his hat in his hand and looked firmly at the ground below, Derek laid out his plan. When he had finished, the men both nodded in agreement without raising their eyes (they were both hard working fathers, after all), but they insisted that Derek would have to be the one to take action because if they tampered with the coffin they could find themselves being accused of bunking. Grave robbing watchmen? Sadly, it wouldn't be the first murmur of it happening. The three men were more than aware that murmurs usually led to lynching. Derek agreed to their terms -it would be a solo act.

Now it was 4 am and the funeral felt like a lifetime ago. The rain had temporarily stopped - a long overdue break - but the ground was still soft as Derek dug into the moist earth with the old, stained spade he had retrieved from behind the small watchtower. The half-moon shone down on him as he stood, spade in hand, in a trench digging down until he reached the wooden coffin that just twelve hours earlier had been lowered with the blessing of the minister. With an almighty heave, he opened the coffin lid and a loud creek broke the silence. Derek looked inside the wooden carton, which was the part he had been dreading most. Thankfully the smell was no worse than he had imagined. He tried not to look at the deformed face of his lifeless young son lying there in his Sunday best. Wiping a tear from his eye, he opened up his canvas bag and pulled out a collection of wires. He tied them around the side of the coffin and around Jimmy's body. Squatting now, he clipped each wire into place with putty and pushed it gently against the wooden sides, using his thumb and forefinger against each other. Cautiously, Derek took another smaller bag from his larger one, unclipped it and began to prudently pour its contents around his son's head. The gunpowder lay in between his ears and the coffin walls. But some scattered over his child's face. Being careful to avoid the eyes, mouth and nostrils, Derek continued to empty the bag. As the rain began to fall again, he gently placed the empty bag back into the larger one and returned the coffin lid, cutting off the few loose wires underneath it with an old pair of pliers. He then carefully placed the pliers under the wire cut offs into his canvas bag. In the darkness of the night, Derek was sure the grave robbers wouldn't see his booby trap. Wiping a dirty hand over his face and removing his cap, he quickly said a quiet prayer and began the job of placing the Earth back onto the coffin. As he worked, he occasionally looked over his shoulder in case some of the newly appointed Dundee Police Force saw the movement or even worse, members of the general public.

They would certainly take him for a grave robber. Things were so bad that people often decided to take the law into their own hands, and the last thing poor, suffering Margaret needed was a lynch mob tearing her husband from limb to limb.

After twenty long, dark and cold minutes, Derek flattened the earth and placed the spade behind the nearest gravestone, so the watchmen could find and remove it as soon as he signalled to them. He looked again at his son's gravestone, which read;

Secret to the memory of James. M McCaw, aged only six years. He died of Cholera, 13th July 1823. This monument is erected by a few of his numerous friends as a mark of their affectionate regard and esteem and of the deep regret they felt at his untimely and sudden death.

Derek placed his cap firmly on his head and walked back the way he came, clutching the bag slung over his shoulder tightly as he climbed over the cemetery wall. He whistled as he did so, giving Alistair and Freddie the signal to keep a steady watch now that his vigilante act was complete.

Derek walked home through the cobbled streets of Meadowside. He quietly let himself into the house, took off his dirty boots, placed his jacket and hat onto a chair, shoved his bag under the table so that the evidence could be removed the following day, and let out a large sigh. Then he got into bed next to his sobbing wife and gently held her hand below the bed sheet. When sleep finally found him, Derek dreamt of opened graves, of resurrections, of walking skeletons and of decaying flesh. He dreamt of baying mobs and diarrhoea, of disease and destruction of flesh. His nightmares had become as dark as the world outside.

Before morning came, he was awakened by the noise of a loud blast.

"What was that Derek?" asked Margaret, wiping her eyes. "it sounded like an explosion. Was it the factory?"

"Nothing, dear. Go back to sleep," Derek replied as a tear rolled down his dirty cheek and onto the pillow below.

Printed in Great Britain
by Amazon

22475059R00096